In the middle of the rocky tunnel, right in front of them, was a gaping hole. The stone around it was disintegrating, as if some prehistoric monster had bitten it in anger. The hole opened onto a chasm. It was so deep that drops of water fell down it without making a sound.

Selenia slid down the spider's front leg and stopped in front of a wooden sign next to the hole. It was marked: NO ENTRY. To be sure that this instruction would be clear even to those who couldn't read very well, a skull and crossbones was drawn above the words.

"It's here," said the princess.

ALSO BY LUC BESSON

Arthur and the Minimoys

LUC BESSON
ARTHUR
and the
FORBIDDEN CITY

FROM AN ORIGINAL IDEA BY
CÉLINE GARCIA

TRANSLATED BY ELLEN SOWCHEK

HarperTrophy®

An Imprint of HarperCollinsPublishers

Arthur and the Forbidden City
Copyright © 2005 by Intervista

Library of Congress Cataloging-in-Publication Data
Besson, Luc.
[Arthur et la cité interdite. English]
Arthur and the forbidden city / by Luc Besson ; based on
an original idea by Céline Garcia ; translated by Ellen
Sowchek.— 1st American ed.
p. cm.
"Originally published in France under the title Arthur et
la cité interdite by Intervista/Manitoba in 2003."
Sequel to: Arthur and the Minimoys.
Summary: In order to find his grandfather's lost treasure
and save the Minimoys, Arthur and his companions, includ-
ing Princess Selenia, travel into the forbidden city ruled by
Maltazard the Cursed.
ISBN-10: 0-06-059628-7 — ISBN-13: 978-0-06-059628-6
[1. Grandparent and child—Fiction. 2. Magic—Fiction.
3. Buried treasure—Fiction. 4. Adventure and adventurers—
Fiction. 5. Size—Fiction. 6. Kings, queens, rulers, etc.—Fiction.
7. Fantasy.] I. Sowchek, Ellen. II. Title.
PZ7.B46565Ar 2005   2004027651
[Fic]—dc22   CIP
                                                              AC

Typography by Karin Paprocki
❖
First Harper Trophy edition, 2006
First American Edition, 2005
Originally published in France under the title
Arthur et la cité interdite by Intervista/Manitoba in 2003

ARTHUR
and the
FORBIDDEN CITY

CHAPTER

1

As the sun sank slowly over the peaceful valley, Alfred the dog opened one eye. A slight breeze signaled that the temperature might finally be bearable. He got up slowly, stretched his legs, emerged from the shadow of the windmill where he had been hiding, and trotted across the grass.

From the tall chimney of the house by the river, a young sparrow hawk followed the dog with its piercing eyes, but only for a few seconds. That prey was too large. The bird turned its head slowly, looking for another victim. Suddenly it let out a hoarse, powerful cry that awakened Grandma, who was stretched out on the couch in the living room.

Grandma sat upright. "How could I doze off like that?" she asked herself, rubbing her eyes. The events of the last few days came back to her. Arthur, her adored only grandson, had disappeared—just as her husband had done four years earlier, in the garden by the oak tree in search of a treasure.

She had searched the garden from one end to the other,

torn the house apart, and called for him from all the neigh-boring hills, without finding a trace of her grandson.

She imagined so many different explanations . . . perhaps extraterrestrials, for one. She imagined large green men coming down from the sky in their UFO and kidnapping Arthur. She was almost sure of it.

She missed his little blond head, tousled hair, and two large brown eyes, always with their look of wonder. She missed his voice, as sweet and fragile as a soap bubble. A tear made its lonely way down her cheek.

She looked at the sky for a moment through the window. It was uniformly blue and desperately empty. No trace of extra-terrestrials. She let out a long sigh and looked around her at the silent house.

It was lucky that the sparrow hawk had woken her up. The coolness of the room and the hypnotic tick-tock of the clock had made it impossible to resist taking a nap.

The young bird of prey cried again.

Grandma perked up her ears. She was ready to interpret anything as a sign, a mark of hope. She was convinced that the sparrow hawk had seen or heard something, and she wasn't entirely wrong. The bird was indeed declaring that he had heard something even before it was visible on the horizon.

That something was a car, accompanied by a cloud of dust that glistened in the sunlight. The sparrow hawk scrutinized the car from the chimney top as if he were equipped with radar.

Grandma listened carefully. She could hear a faint rumbling in the distance.

The sparrow hawk let out two small cries, as if to indicate the number of passengers inside the car.

Grandma turned her head slightly, the way you would turn an antenna in order to capture a signal. The engine noise could suddenly be heard everywhere, and the trees began to stir, echoing its horrible sound.

The sparrow hawk decided it was time to leave, which was not a good sign. Perhaps he could sense the series of events that was about to take place.

Grandma jumped to her feet. There was no doubt about it—the sparrow hawk had sent her a signal. Grandma composed herself, straightened her dress over her considerable frame, and searched frantically for her slippers.

The noise of the engine invaded the living room. Grandma stopped her search and headed toward the door wearing only one slipper, limping like an old pirate with a wooden leg.

The engine stopped. The door of the car squealed as it opened, and two worn leather shoes emerged, stepping onto the gravel. Grandma reached the door and struggled with the key.

"Why on earth did I lock the door?" she grumbled to herself, her head down. She did not notice the two silhouettes outlined by the sun behind the door.

The key rattled a little but finally turned in the lock. Grandma was so surprised by what she saw as the door swung open that she could not help letting out a little cry of horror.

There was nothing particularly horrible about the smiling couple standing on the landing, except perhaps their bad taste. The lady was wearing a dress with large purple flowers, the man a plaid jacket of greenish yellow. It was hard on the eyes but nothing to scream about.

Grandma stifled her cry and tried to convert it into a welcoming noise.

"Surprise!" chanted the couple, in perfect unison.

Grandma spread her arms and tried as best she could to assume a natural-looking smile. Her mouth said Hello while her eyes said Help.

"What a surprise," she ended up blurting out. Arthur's parents were standing in front of her, as real as a nightmare.

Grandma continued to smile, blocking the front door like a soccer goalie.

Since Grandma was not moving, not speaking, but only stood there with her strange smile, Arthur's father was forced to ask the question that she feared the most.

"Is Arthur here?" he asked jovially, without a moment's

doubt about what the answer would be.

Grandma smiled some more, as if hoping to suggest a positive answer without actually lying. But Arthur's father was waiting for a reply. So Grandma took a breath and said, "Did you have a good trip?"

This was not really the answer that Arthur's father was waiting for, but he was a good driver, so he launched into a detailed account. "We took the shortcut to the west," he explained. "The roads are narrow there, but according to my calculations we saved about twenty-five miles. Which means, given the price of a gallon of gas, that we—"

"That we had to turn every three seconds for two hours," complained Arthur's mother. "The trip was a horror and I am grateful that Arthur did not have to suffer such punishment." Then she added, "So where is he?"

"Who?" asked Grandma, as if she were hearing voices.

"Arthur. My son," the younger woman answered, somewhat concerned—not for her son but for the mental state of her mother. Could it be the heat? she wondered.

"Aaah! . . . He is going to be so happy to see you," Grandma offered as a reply.

Arthur's parents looked at each other, wondering if perhaps the old lady had finally gone deaf.

"Arthur. Where is he?" Arthur's father repeated slowly, making his words very distinct.

Grandma smiled once more and nodded.

This answer convinced no one, and she finally had to say something. "He is . . . with the dog," she said. This was just at the edge of lying, but the answer seemed to satisfy the couple.

At that exact moment, Alfred decided to make an appearance, wagging his tail and instantly destroying this perfect alibi.

Grandma's smile crumbled.

"All right, Mom. Where is he?" Arthur's mother asked in a much firmer tone of voice.

Grandma would have gladly strangled Alfred, but she contented herself with giving him a sharp look. "So, are you and Arthur playing hide-and-seek?" she asked Alfred a little too sweetly.

Alfred seemed to understand what Grandma was saying. His tail gradually slowed down. He knew that he had probably done something stupid and was already pleading guilty.

"They love to play hide-and-seek, those two," Grandma explained. "They could play for days! Arthur hides and—"

"And the dog counts to a hundred?" Arthur's father replied, wondering whether he was the victim of a huge practical joke.

"Yes, that's it! Alfred counts up to one hundred and then he looks for Arthur!"

The parents looked at each other with great concern. Had

Grandma finally gone off her rocker?

"And . . . do you have an idea where Arthur might be hiding?" Arthur's father asked gently.

Grandma nodded her head energetically. "Yes! In the garden!"

Never had a lie been so close to the truth.

CHAPTER
2

Deep in the garden, sliding along immense blades of grass where the roots of trees were born, was the bottom of an old wall built by the hand of man.

In this wall, eaten away by time, was a small crevice that ran between the stones. When you are barely half an inch tall, this is an impressive chasm, a very deep hole, which our heroes were rapidly approaching.

Princess Selenia was in the lead, as usual. She had lost none of her strength, and their mission seemed to occupy all her thoughts. She walked along the path as if she were strolling down Main Street, totally unaware of the absolute void that bordered the route on either side.

Behind her, always staying close, was Arthur. He was still fascinated by everything that was happening to him. Arthur, who, a day or so earlier, had felt bad about being less than five feet tall, was now proud of his half-inch stature. And he thanked his lucky stars every moment for this adventure.

He breathed deeply, as if to take better advantage of his luck. At this point, it should be mentioned that Arthur's eyes were not so much on the chasm as on Selenia.

It should also be mentioned that Selenia was very pretty. Even from behind you could tell she was a princess. In any event, that's what could be seen in Arthur's look, as he followed her like Alfred the dog. Back when he was a normal height and on the other side of the garden, he had seen a picture of her in one of his grandfather's books. He still couldn't believe he was having a real adventure with her.

Betameche, Selenia's brother, lagged behind. He still had his backpack, filled with thousands of things, all of which were useless except in weighing him down so he wouldn't fly away.

"Beta, come on! Time is wasting," his sister called out in the grumpy way she always spoke to him.

Betameche let out a huge sigh. "I'm tired of carrying everything," he complained.

"No one asked you to bring half the village," the princess replied acidly.

"We could each take a turn carrying, couldn't we? That way I could rest a little, and we could move faster," Betameche offered.

Selenia came to a sudden stop and looked at her brother. "You're right. We'll save time. Give it to me!"

Betameche took off his backpack and handed it to his sister who, in one swift movement, threw it into the abyss.

"There! Now you will be less tired and we will travel faster," the princess announced. "Let's go!"

Betameche watched in horror as his backpack disappeared into the bottomless void. He couldn't believe his eyes.

Arthur had no intention of involving himself in this family quarrel. He suddenly became very interested in the crystals covering the wall.

Betameche was seething.

"You are nothing but—but a little *pest!*" he cried.

Selenia just smiled. "The 'little pest' has a mission to accomplish that cannot be delayed. If the pace is too much for you, you can go home! There you can tell all your stories and be fussed over by the king!"

"At least our father has a heart," Betameche retorted.

"Yes, he does, and you had better take advantage of it, because the next king will not have one!"

"Who is the next king?" asked Arthur timidly.

"The next king . . . is me," said Selenia proudly, lifting her chin.

Arthur was beginning to understand, but some things still confused him. "Is that why you absolutely must get married in the next two days?" he asked.

"Yes. The prince must be chosen *before* I assume my duties as sovereign. That's the way it is. That's the rule," answered Selenia, speaking faster in order to avoid more questions.

Arthur let out a sigh. If only he had more time. He needed time to know whether this warmth that he was feeling inside his chest, and which often rose to his cheeks, could be considered a sign of love.

Now he understood why Martin, the police officer back home, would get so tongue-tied whenever he flirted with Grandma. In the human world, Arthur was only ten, but by Minimoy standards he was hundreds of years old—old enough, he thought, to be in love and to marry Selenia.

But he needed more time to really understand the word "love." It was a word that was much too big for him.

He loved his grandmother, his dog, their pickup truck . . . but he did not dare to say that he loved Selenia. Besides, all he had to do was think about it, and he started blushing.

"What's wrong with you?" asked the princess, amused.

"Nothing," murmured Arthur, blushing even more. "It's just the heat. It is so hot here!"

Selenia smiled at this lie. She snapped off one of the small stalactites hanging from the wall and handed the piece of ice to Arthur. "Here—rub this on your forehead and you'll feel better."

Arthur thanked her and held the piece of ice to his forehead.

Selenia knew that what he was feeling had nothing to do with the temperature, as it was around freezing in this endless chasm.

The stick of ice melted and Arthur was suddenly overcome

by a burst of courage. "May I ask you a personal question, Selenia?"

"You may always ask. I will decide whether to answer," the princess answered, as shrewd as ever.

"You have to choose a husband in two days but . . . in nearly a thousand years, you haven't found anyone who suited you?" asked Arthur.

"A princess deserves an exceptional being: intelligent, courageous, recklessly brave, a good cook, one who loves children—" she began, as she always did.

"Who knows how to do the housekeeping and the laundry while her ladyship takes a nap," Beta interrupted.

"An exceptional individual, one who understands his wife and protects her, even against the stupidity of certain members of her family," Selenia shot back, fixing an angry look on her brother. And then she began to dream out loud . . .

"A handsome guy, of course, but also true, loyal, with a sense of duty and responsibility. An infallible being, generous and luminous!"

Her eyes met Arthur's. He was beginning to feel a bit ill. Each adjective sounded like the blow of a hammer to his head.

"Not one of those weaklings who can't even handle a little jack-fire," added the princess.

"Of course," Arthur replied, crushed under the weight of unhappiness. How could he have imagined for even a second that he had a chance? Arthur had none of those qualities. He was neither infallible nor luminous, and if he had to describe himself, he would more likely use the words "small," "stupid," and "ugly."

"Choosing a fiancé is the most important thing for a princess. And the first kiss is a crucial moment," Selenia said. "Not because of one's feelings! Here, the act is much more than sym-bolic, because it is during this first kiss that the princess shares all her powers with the prince. Immense powers that will make it possible for him to rule in her absence if necessary. All the peoples of the Seven Lands will owe him allegiance."

Arthur had not actually suspected the importance of this first kiss, and now he understood better why Selenia had to be careful to choose well. "And that's why M. wants to marry you—is that it? For your powers?" he asked.

"No! It's for her great personality!" Betameche joked.

Selenia shrugged. Arthur gave her a long look, ready to forgive her all her faults in exchange for a smile. Anything else seemed impossible. She was too beautiful, too brave, too intelligent, and too much of a princess to be interested in an ordinary boy like him.

"He will never be my husband," Selenia declared like a clap of thunder in a cloudless sky. For a moment, Arthur thought she meant him. He bowed his head, crushed. Selenia glanced at him mischievously.

"I was referring to M. the cursed, obviously," she said.

Arthur felt better, but he wished he could ask her the thousand and one questions that were burning inside him. Despite his efforts to keep them in, one of them ended up escaping.

"When you have to choose your . . . husband, how will you be able to tell the difference between those that are there for your powers and those who really . . . love you?"

There was so much sincerity in the voice of this little boy that even a beautiful, pretentious princess could not be insensitive to it. Perhaps for the first time, she really looked at him, and smiled.

"It is very easy to distinguish between the true and the false, to know which suitor is sincere and which is only there for wealth and power. In fact, I have a test for it." She had let down the bait and she watched Arthur swim around it.

"What—what kind of test?" he asked.

"A test of trust. The one who claims to love me must be able to have complete trust in me. The kind of blind trust that he has in himself. This is generally very difficult for a man," Selenia explained. Her little fish had his mouth open and was ready to bite.

"I trust you, Selenia," Arthur replied, taking the bait—hook, line, and sinker.

Selenia smiled. The little fish was on her line. She stopped and looked at him for a moment. "Really?" she asked, her almond eyes fixed on him, as formidable as those of a serpent.

"Really," Arthur replied.

Selenia's smile widened.

"Is this a marriage proposal?" she asked. It was like a cat sticking its paw into a goldfish bowl.

Arthur turned bright red. "All right . . . I know I'm still a little young . . ." he murmured, "but I did save your life a few times and—"

Selenia interrupted him. "Love is not about protecting someone you do not want to lose! Love is giving everything to the other person—even your life—without hesitating, without even thinking about it!"

Arthur was disturbed. He saw love as something big and powerful, but still undefined. Love for him was a feeling that made him lose his balance. He had not understood how high the stakes were and that, sometimes, it could cost you your life.

"Are you ready to give your life? Out of love for me?" Selenia asked, still mischievous.

Arthur was somewhat lost. There was no way out of this fishbowl—only a slippery wall that let him swim around in circles. "Okay . . . if that is the only way to prove my love . . . yes," he conceded, feeling a bit nervous.

Selenia approached him and walked around him, like a mouse around a piece of cheese. "Good. Let us see if you are telling the truth," she said. "Step back!"

Arthur took one step back, thankful to have passed this first test.

"Step back again," Selenia commanded. Arthur glanced at Betameche, who rolled his eyes and sighed. His sister's games had never amused him.

Arthur hesitated a moment, then took a good step back.

"Step back again," Selenia commanded.

Arthur glanced over his shoulder. There was the cliff edge, the one they had been walking along for hours. It bordered space so deep that it disappeared into absolute darkness.

Arthur now had a better understanding of the test. This was far from a traditional game of Simon Says. But he had set out to prove his courage, so he stepped back again until his heels touched the edge.

Selenia put on a beautiful, satisfied smile. *This little fish is very docile*, she seemed to be thinking, but the test was not over.

"Arthur, I asked you to step back. Why are you stopping? Don't you trust me anymore?"

Arthur was confused. He could not understand the connection between love and trust, the step back, and the chasm that was awaiting him. He suddenly regretted all the times he had slept through math class. Perhaps if he had paid attention, he would now be able to solve this equation.

"Don't you trust me?" insisted Selenia.

"Of course," replied Arthur, "I trust you."

"So why have you stopped?" the princess asked provokingly.

Arthur thought a moment and found his answer. He slowly straightened up, threw out his small chest, and looked Selenia right in the eyes. "I stopped . . . to say good-bye," he said solemnly.

A glimmer of panic appeared in her eyes.

Betameche understood immediately. The poor boy, too honest to play his sister's games, was about to do the unthinkable. "Don't do it, Arthur," Beta stammered, too worried to make the slightest movement toward Arthur.

"Farewell," said Arthur melodramatically.

Selenia's smile collapsed like a house of cards. Her game was turning into a nightmare.

Arthur took a big step back.

"No!" Selenia yelled. She covered her face with her hands.

Arthur disappeared, swallowed up by the endless chasm.

Selenia cried out in despair. She turned away from the chasm and fell to her knees, her face buried in her hands. She could barely understand what had happened.

"With a test like *that* you will never get married,"

said Betameche angrily.

Just then, Arthur appeared in the air behind Selenia, as if he had bounced off something. He did not seem in control of his movements, but he was able to put his fingers to his lips, signaling to Betameche to keep quiet. Astonished, the little Minimoy nodded before Arthur disappeared again.

Selenia, too preoccupied with her unhappiness, had seen nothing.

"You know, when you play with fire, you get burned," said Betameche.

His sister agreed sadly.

Betameche was delighted. Now that he had the chance to punish his sister a bit, he had to rub salt into the wound. "How can you call yourself a princess when you let your most ardent suitor die?"

"How could I do that?" cried Selenia, moved to sincerity. "How could I be so stupid and so mean at the same time? I thought I was a princess and then I behaved like the most selfish girl in the world! I don't deserve my name or my rank! No punishment will ever make up for my guilt!"

"Yes, I can't think of anything that would," agreed Betameche, as Arthur appeared again, in an even stranger position.

"Oh, I am proud and cruel," the princess sobbed. "I believed that he was not worthy of me, when it was I who was not worthy of him. My head sacrificed him but my heart chose him."

"Really?" said Betameche.

"From the first moment I saw him," confessed Selenia between sobs. "He was so cute, with his big brown eyes and his lost expression. Gentleness and beauty lit up his face, while his posture breathed nobility. His step was graceful, light—"

Arthur bounced back again in the most shocking contortion yet, calling to mind a disjointed puppet.

"He was kind, brilliant, daring—" said the princess.

"Charming?" asked Arthur, mid-somersault.

"Yes, the most charming of all the princes that the Seven Lands have ever known. He was charming, brave—" She stopped cold. Where had that question come from? She whirled around and saw Arthur bounce into view, upside down.

"Charming, brave, what else?" he asked, delighted with so many compliments.

Anger appeared instantly on Selenia's face. She looked like a teakettle ready to whistle. "And—a real smooth talker!" she cried in a voice so loud it flipped him right side up.

Arthur disappeared again as Selenia approached the edge to find out the secret of his survival.

Arthur was bouncing off a giant spiderweb that was

woven from one side of the precipice to the other. His fall had been without danger and his exit purely theatrical. But Selenia did not appreciate the drama. He wouldn't get away with this treachery. She unsheathed her sword and waited for Arthur's return.

"You are the most manipulative person I know," she yelled, as he twisted aside to avoid being struck by her sword. "You'll see there is a price to pay when you play with the feelings of a princess!"

"Selenia, if everyone who loves you has to kill himself in order to prove it, you will never find a husband," Arthur replied sensibly.

"He is right," added Betameche, always ready to throw a little more oil on the fire.

Selenia turned around and, with a single swing of her sword, sliced off the three rebellious hairs on top of Betameche's head.

"You've been his accomplice right from the start! You are a terrible brother!" Selenia snapped. And the two began to squabble, to the amusement of Arthur who had finally figured out how to control his bouncing.

The spiderweb was sturdy enough to hold him, but on the far side there was a thread that shook slightly with each rebound. These small, regular vibrations ran the length of the thread and were carried through a cavern.

The thread then disappeared into the darkness. It was a darkness much more dense than that inside the void, and also more disturbing.

But curiosity being stronger than fear, we cannot stop from entering this cave or following this thread into the darkness. Where we will soon find two shapes—two eyes. Red. Filled with blood.

Arthur was laughing now, unaware of the danger. "Come on, Selenia! Forgive me," he called on another of his rebounds. "Yes, I knew that there was a spiderweb, but I still listened to you, didn't I? I'm just lucky this web was here!"

Selenia was not interested in games or even in words. She was thinking more along the lines of a good spanking for this impudent knave.

But the punishment she was imagining would come on its own. All at once, Arthur's acrobatics came to a sudden stop. He had gotten his leg caught between the threads of the web.

This changed the nature of the vibration, a change that communicated itself along the thread and into the cave. The two red eyes that lived there seemed to appreciate the news, and the spider began to advance.

When you are less than an inch tall, you see life from a different perspective. What seemed to a human to be a gentle little spider, now appeared to be a veritable tank with eight legs, as furry as a woolly mammoth's. She stretched her face full of stingers and slobbered a little. In spider language, this was what passed for a smile.

The large mandibles began to move along the thread as the creature stalked toward its web.

CHAPTER
3

"What do you mean 'disappeared'?" Arthur's mother exclaimed, sinking down on the sofa. Arthur's father sat down next to his wife and put his arm around her shoulders.

Grandma was making knots with her fingers, like a school-girl with a bad report card. "I don't know where to begin," murmured the old lady.

"Perhaps you should start at the beginning," Arthur's father suggested.

Grandma cleared her throat. She wasn't feeling very comfortable in front of this audience. "Well, the day Arthur got here, the weather was very nice. The water in the river was particularly warm and Arthur wanted to go fishing. So we took his grandfather's fishing poles and left on an adventure which, in reality, went no farther than the garden's edge."

The audience of two did not move, and there were only two explanations for that: either they were captivated by Arthur's fishing adventure, or they were dismayed to see Grandma so shamelessly trying to buy time.

"You cannot imagine how many fish that little guy can catch in one hour! Come on, guess," Grandma demanded with enthusiasm.

Arthur's parents looked at each other, not wondering about the number of fish their charming son was able to catch but rather how much longer Grandma would try to stall.

"Would you please get to the details of our son's disappearance?" asked Arthur's father.

The old woman sighed.

Her grandson had disappeared. They had to accept this painful reality.

She sat on the edge of an armchair, as if not to disturb it. "Every night I tell Arthur about Africa, using his grandfather's books and travel journals. They are of course very informative, but Archibald was a poet so his books are also full of tales and legends. Arthur especially liked the story of the Bogo-Matassalai and their little friends, the miniature Minimoys," Grandma said with a tremor in her voice. Speaking about her missing husband was always difficult. It had been four years since he disappeared, and it still seemed like yesterday.

"What does that have to do with Arthur's disappearance?" her son-in-law asked drily, bringing Grandma back from her reverie.

"Well . . . Arthur became convinced that not only do the

Minimoys exist but that they live in the garden," Grandma concluded.

Arthur's parents looked at her with disbelief. "In the garden?" repeated Arthur's father, who needed a confirmation of this rubbish.

Grandma nodded.

Arthur's father collected his thoughts, which took only a moment. "All right. Let's imagine there are Minimoys in the garden. What does that have to do with Arthur's disappearance?" he asked.

"Well, unfortunately, Mr. Davido arrived while we were having birthday cake. You know how quick Arthur is at understanding things," Grandma said.

"Who is this Davido? And what was he doing with the cake?" asked Arthur's father, feeling that the conversation was getting away from him.

"Mr. Ernest Davido is the landlord. Arthur quickly realized that we are having some money problems. In fact, if I don't pay Mr. Davido the money we owe very soon, the house and land will belong to him. Arthur decided that he had to find the treasure that his grandpa hid, to help me," the old woman explained.

"What treasure?" asked Arthur's father, suddenly taking a real interest in the story.

"Rubies, I think. They were a gift from the Bogo-Matassalai, and Archibald buried them somewhere in the garden."

"In the garden?" Arthur's father repeated again. He seemed able to retain only what interested him.

"Yes, but the garden is quite big. That's why Arthur wanted to find the Minimoys, so they could guide him to the treasure," concluded Grandma. It all seemed perfectly logical to her.

Arthur's father paused for a moment, like a dog in front of a rabbit hole. "Do you have a shovel?" he asked, with a gleam in his eye.

It was almost nightfall. Magnificent streaks of navy blue crossed the sky. The headlights of the parents' car were two points of yellow light illuminating the garden. From time to time, a shovel would poke out of a hole and throw its contents aside.

Occasionally, another shovel, slower and less full, would also appear.

Grandma sat on the steps opposite the garden that was no longer a garden. It looked like a battlefield. There were holes everywhere, as if a giant mole had gone mad. And there was the mole now, sticking its head out with a yelp. It had just broken its shovel.

In fact, it was Arthur's father, who was barely recognizable with his face covered in dirt. "How are we supposed to do this with such rotten equipment?" he exclaimed, angrily tossing the shovel handle aside.

His wife emerged from the neighboring hole. "Dear, calm

down. There is no use in getting angry," she said soothingly.

"Give me your shovel," Arthur's father said grumpily. He practically grabbed the tool from her hands, dove into his hole, and began working even harder.

Grandma was sorry, as sorry as her garden was now. Despite her usual good humor, she was beginning to feel depressed.

"What's the use of finding the treasure if Arthur is not here to take advantage of it?" she asked.

Arthur's father reappeared. "Don't worry, Grandma. He's probably just lost, that's all. But I know my son. He can manage. I am sure that he will find his way home. Since he's always hungry, he will most likely be back by dinnertime," he added, thinking he was being reassuring.

"It's ten o'clock at night," Grandma said, looking at her watch.

Arthur's father looked up and noticed that it was already well into the night.

"What? Oh, yes, that's true," he said, amazed at how fast time flies when you are looking for buried treasure. "No problem, then he'll go directly to bed. That way we can save on one meal," he joked.

"Francis," Arthur's mother said angrily. Her vocabulary sometimes seemed limited to this word, which she always used with the same tone of annoyance.

"Oh, it's all right. I was just joking," Arthur's father said. "As a matter of fact, though . . . I am a little bit hungry myself right now."

"All I have is what's left of Arthur's birthday cake," Grandma offered. "We'll have to eat it by candlelight, since our electricity was turned off when we couldn't pay our bill."

"Perfect," said Arthur's father, thinking more of the cake than of the electric bill. "Since we weren't there when it was served, we can have it now!"

"*Francis*," complained Arthur's mother, following them inside.

CHAPTER
4

Arthur was having a hard time freeing himself from his trap. The threads were covered with a slightly sticky substance that did not help matters, and he became increasingly more entangled.

"You've got to help me, Selenia!" he called, loud enough to be heard on the path above.

"Why?" Selenia replied, secretly pleased at his predicament. She figured no real harm would come to him and thought that it might teach him a lesson. "This will give you time to think about what you've done!"

"I haven't *done* anything!" Arthur shouted. "I just did what you asked and had a little bit of luck. That's all. Don't be angry with me for that. And, besides, everything you said about me was very nice!"

"I didn't mean any of it!" replied the princess.

Betameche spoke up. "Oh, really? Then why did you say it? Now you just say things that you don't mean?"

"No, I always mean what I say," murmured Selenia, "but

this time, it was different. I was motivated by remorse and guilt. I would have said anything to soothe my conscience."

"So you lied?" insisted Beta.

"No, I never lie," Selenia snapped back, feeling more and more as if she were in a trap. "Both of you get on my nerves. Okay! I'm not perfect. Are you happy now?"

"Yes, I am," replied Betameche, delighted by this confession.

"I'm not," said Arthur, who had just noticed the spider. Even though she was impressive, it was not her size or her appearance that frightened Arthur—it was the direction she was taking. The creature was heading straight for him and most certainly not to say hello. More likely, it would be good-bye!

"Now what are you complaining about?" Selenia asked as she leaned toward Arthur. "Perhaps you think *you're* perfect?"

"Not at all! Quite the contrary. I think I am small, stuck, and completely powerless! And I am really in need of help," answered Arthur, beginning to panic.

"That's a nice confession. A little late, of course, but good to hear," the princess added.

The spider continued along her route, following the thread that was leading directly to Arthur.

"Selenia, help! A giant spider is heading straight for me," cried Arthur.

Princess Selenia glanced at the spider. "This spider is a perfectly normal size! Must you always exaggerate?" commented the princess, completely unimpressed.

"Selenia, she is going to eat me!" screamed the young man, completely panicked.

Selenia knelt on the ground and leaned over the edge a little, as if to make their conversation more intimate.

"I would have preferred that you die of shame, but . . . eaten by a spider is not too bad, either!" she said with a note of humor that only she seemed to find funny.

She got up with a big smile.

"Farewell," she said lightly, and disappeared.

Arthur was at the mercy of the monster. Abandoned, petrified, liquefied. In a word, already dead. The spider would have licked her chops, if she had any.

"Selenia, I will never make fun of you again. I swear it on the Seven Lands and on my life!" begged Arthur, but his pleas went nowhere. The edge of the chasm where Selenia had been was now desperately empty. She was gone.

Arthur was crushed. For having toyed with the feelings of a princess, he was going to die, eaten by this creature with eight hairy legs. He struggled, but to no avail. Every movement only made him more stuck and more entangled, and he was rapidly losing strength. He was tied up like a piece of meat, ready to be put into the oven.

"Selenia, I beg of you, I will do anything you want," he cried in a last burst of hope.

The head of the princess appeared, like a jack-in-the-box springing out. She was right above him, on the other side. "You promise never to make fun of Her Royal Highness again?" she asked slyly.

Arthur was at his wit's end and in no position to negotiate. "Yes, I promise! Now, quick, untangle me!" Arthur pleaded.

Selenia did not seem in much of a hurry.

"Yes who?" she asked.

"Yes, Your Highness," said Arthur anxiously.

"Your what Highness?" she insisted.

"Yes, Your Royal Highness!" Arthur cried.

Selenia hesitated for a moment. "Deal," she said, holding up her chin as only princesses know how.

The spider was on them, her large mouth open wide.

Arthur would have liked to scream, but he was paralyzed with fear and no sound would come out.

Selenia stood up, turned around, and slugged the spider. The creature stopped dead in her tracks, groggy. The beast waved her head from side to side and realized that her jaw was now making a strange sound. The little princess had struck hard, and it was now sounding like a machine that had lost its nuts and bolts.

It wasn't only the spider that was speechless. Arthur's mouth was wide open. He couldn't believe his eyes. Selenia had just punched a spider in the nose! A few hours earlier, this vision would have seemed totally crazy to him—something that would make his mother send him to bed with two aspirins.

Selenia snapped her fingers in the direction of Betameche, who was perched on a small rock nearby, watching.

"Beta—lollipop, please!" ordered the princess.

Betameche rummaged through his pockets and took out a small, perfectly round lollipop wrapped in beautiful rose petals. He threw the lollipop to his sister, who caught it with one hand. With the other, she removed the wrapper, and the lollipop immediately blew up to an enormous size, like an air bag.

"Here, this will make you feel better," promised Selenia, stuffing the large pink bubble into the spider's mouth.

The creature froze and squinted at the stick coming out of her mouth as if she did not know quite what to do.

"Go on. It's grape," Selenia said.

At this, the spider stopped hesitating and began to lick it. Her blood-red eyes gradually turned a deeper color, the color of grapes, and became almond-shaped.

Selenia smiled at her. "Good girl," she told her, before returning to Arthur, still tangled up in the web. She took out her sword and cut the threads to free him.

"You saved my life and now I've saved yours. We are even," said Selenia as if she were announcing the results of a contest.

"You saved nothing," said Arthur rebelliously. "You knew from the beginning that I was in no danger. You left me hanging so that I would make you promises!"

"You knew that you weren't in danger, too! You looked behind you and saw that there was a spiderweb that would break your fall! But you wanted to mess with me and so you were caught in your own trap!" replied Selenia, whose voice had gone up a note.

"This from her ladyship, who plays at being an iron princess and who cries like a fountain when she loses her good-for-nothing friend!" Arthur retorted, getting a little annoyed.

"You know, you two make quite a couple," Betameche said with a laugh. "At least you will never get bored with each other!"

"Mind your own business!" Selenia and Arthur replied in unison.

"You claimed you would die for me and all you did was make fun of me. You are nothing but a dirty liar!" the princess continued to Arthur.

"Oh yeah? Well, *you* are nothing but a—"

Selenia stopped him in mid-sentence. "Have you already forgotten the promise that you just made to me?"

Arthur grimaced. How did he keep falling into these traps? "I made that promise under the threats of danger and fear," he defended himself.

"It's still a promise, isn't it?"

"Yes," Arthur conceded, somewhat reluctantly.

"Yes, who?" Selenia asked.

Arthur let out a big sigh.

"Yes, Your Royal Highness," he answered, looking down at his shoes.

"At last," she rejoiced. She ran lightly over and climbed up the front leg of the spider, mounting her as if she were a horse. "Let's go," she called.

Betameche jumped from rock to rock and clambered up the length of the creature's leg. He sat behind his sister, very happy that they were finally using a good vehicle. The creature's thick fur made it possible to settle in quite comfortably.

"Well, are you coming?" Betameche called to Arthur, who was so astonished that he still hadn't moved. In less than five minutes, he had gone from nearly being eaten by a giant spider to riding her like a camel!

All it took was a princess with a quick right hook and an inflatable lollipop to make the creature more docile than a little puppy. Even Alice, sometime resident of Wonderland, might already have had a nervous breakdown at this.

"Come on, hurry up! We have lost a lot of time!" Selenia called. "Or would you perhaps prefer running behind, like a faithful miloo?"

Arthur didn't know what a miloo looked like, but he could imagine what kind of domestic animal could easily run alongside a car. He summoned all his courage and grasped the front leg and hair of the spider. He climbed the length of this post, grabbed the fur, and nestled himself in behind Betameche's back.

"Let's go, my beauty!" Selenia cried, pressing her heels into the animal's sides. The spider promptly began to move along the edge of the precipice, just like a faithful donkey in the Grand Canyon.

CHAPTER
5

The spider's rhythmic motion had awakened the young prince's stomach. "I am starving to death!" exclaimed Betameche for the fifth time in as many minutes.

"Just tell us when you are *not* hungry, Betameche. That will be more helpful," his sister answered.

"It's not a crime to be hungry, is it? We haven't eaten for ages!" grumbled the young prince, who was holding on to his stomach as if it were going to run off and join another, more understanding, body. "And since I'm a growing boy, that means I have to eat a lot, doesn't it?"

"You can grow up later, when we're back home," said Selenia, cutting the conversation short.

In the middle of the rocky tunnel, right in front of them, was a gaping hole. The stone around it was disintegrating, as if some prehistoric monster had bitten it in anger. The hole opened onto a chasm. It was so deep that drops of water fell down it without making a sound.

Selenia slid down the spider's front leg and stopped in front of a wooden sign next to the hole. It was marked: NO ENTRY. To be sure that this instruction would be clear even to those who couldn't read very well, a skull and crossbones was drawn above the words.

"It's here," said the princess.

Betameche swallowed nervously. Arthur got down from the spider and approached the hole to look down.

There was nothing to see. Nothing.

"Isn't there another entrance—maybe something a bit more welcoming?" Betameche asked.

"This is the main entrance," the princess answered, not at all fazed by the gaping hole. If this terrifying hole was the main entrance, Arthur could only imagine what the back entrance was like.

Arthur was beginning to think that he had lived through so many magical adventures in the last twenty-four hours that one more seemed routine. He had definitely decided not to ask any more questions. Besides, the one thing in the world that he had been most afraid of was confessing his love to the princess. Now that he had gotten that over with, he was no longer afraid of anyone or anything, not because this confession had given him wings but simply because all the rest, from now on, could not possibly be as terrifying as that one action.

The princess grabbed the spider and led it toward the

gaping hole. "Go on, big girl! Spin us a beautiful thread that will take us down to the bottom," the princess urged gently, scratching her under the chin. The spider half closed her large almond eyes as if she were about to purr. A long silvery thread came out of her and spiraled down into the opening.

Betameche did not find this flimsy ladder reassuring.

"If they wrote 'no entry' and took the trouble of adding a skull and crossbones to it, that should certainly tell us something, shouldn't it?"

"It's a standard greeting here," replied the princess maliciously.

"A standard greeting! They must not have many visitors!" Betameche retorted.

Selenia was becoming annoyed. She was fed up with his little nasal voice making comments at every step. "Would you have preferred: 'Welcome to Necropolis, its palace, its army, and its private prison'?"

At this response, the prince clamped his mouth shut.

"Yes, that sign means 'welcome to the city of death.' Follow me only if you have enough courage to fight," Selenia concluded, before catching the thread between her knees and slipping down into the darkness.

Very quickly, the woosh of her leggings against the thread faded and finally disappeared.

Betameche peered over the edge, but his sister's silhouette was no longer visible. "Perhaps I will stay and guard the spider. I am afraid she might leave if she's left alone," he said nervously.

"As you wish," said Arthur, seizing the thread. He crossed his legs around the cord, as he had learned in school, and prepared to descend.

"That way," Betameche said, as if to cover his cowardice, "when you come back we can make the return trip on her and we will be home sooner!"

"If we come back!" Arthur noted.

"Yes, of course, if you come back!" added Betameche with a wan smile. The idea of returning alone did not seem to enchant him either.

Arthur began to slide down the thread spun by the spider. In a few seconds his silhouette also disappeared into the impenetrable darkness.

A shiver ran through Betameche. No way in the world was he going to slide down that thread. He stood up and sighed with relief, believing he had escaped the worst.

Except that the atmosphere around him was not any more reassuring. There were traces of moisture on the walls. These magnified the echo of far-off cries, distorted by distance . . . endless cries of pain.

Betameche turned around to see what was behind him. He thought he saw something on the far wall. Despite the fear that was gripping his stomach, he moved a few steps closer to see what it might be.

There were images carved into the wall that were shining, thanks to the water that was dripping down them. They were skulls and crossbones, sometimes accompanied by the appropriate skeleton.

Betameche took a few steps back and stepped on a bone, which made a loud cracking sound. The young prince finally noticed that he was in the middle of hundreds of bones, like an open-air cemetery. He let out a cry of horror that went on to mix with the echoes in the back of the cave.

Beta turned to face the spider. "Listen, I really like you, but I shouldn't leave the other two all alone. They will get into trouble without me," he explained.

Betameche grabbed the thread and did not even take the time to cross his legs around it. All he wanted now was to make a fast escape from this unhappy place.

"Anything has to be better than this," he told himself, and leaped out into this black hole that swallowed all light.

Arthur's father was still in his own hole. Overcome with fatigue, he'd fallen asleep on his shovel.

The rhythm of the shovel's movement had slowed way down. Now you would need an appointment to spot a shovel, half full, coming out of the hole to be emptied. This treasure was not ready to be found, it seemed. And Alfred the dog wasn't exactly helping—he'd gone back and was now systematically filling in all the holes.

This was not really done out of a sense of solidarity but rather to prevent anyone from discovering *his* treasure: a dozen marrow bones he had patiently put aside, being the thrifty dog that he is.

Arthur's mother came out of the house with a tray in her hand. She had prepared a pitcher full of ice water and a small place setting on which she had carefully arranged peeled orange sections.

"Darling," she sang as she advanced carefully over this mined territory.

Even with the moon to guide her, the poor woman could not see much. She should have put on her glasses, but her natural vanity often prevented her from wearing them in public. This vanity would cost her dearly, since she did not see the dog's tail, or the impending catastrophe that went along with it. She stepped directly on Alfred's tail, which immediately set him howling.

Arthur's mother shrieked and lost her balance. She teetered forward one step, then one step back, and then fell into the very hole her husband was sleeping in.

The pitcher slid on the tray and, with surprising reflexes, she managed to grab it by the handle. She saved the pitcher, but not its contents. Her husband caught the ice water right in the face. He, in turn, howled inhumanly and began to fight off the ice cubes which were flying everywhere, primarily down his shirt.

Alfred grimaced. He did not like water either, especially not when it was as cold as this was.

"How could you be so clumsy?" Arthur's father shouted. "Can't you pay attention?"

Arthur's mother did not know how to apologize. She collected the ice cubes, now covered with dirt, and put them back into the pitcher, as if that would do any good.

Grandma appeared on the front steps, another tray in her hands. "I brought you some hot coffee!" she offered.

Arthur's father waved his arms frantically. After the ice cubes, he was not at all thrilled about the prospect of receiving a cup of hot coffee in his face.

"Don't move," he cried, as if Grandma were about to step on a snake. "Put it down there and I'll come and get it a little later," he added.

Grandma did not know what to think. She knew that her daughter had married an eccentric, but here she must have missed a chapter. She shrugged, put the tray down on the steps, and went back into the house without saying a word.

Arthur's mother tried to sponge off her husband with her delicate little silk handkerchief. It was like trying to empty a bathtub with a straw. Grumbling, he climbed out of the hole and headed for the house. His wife followed him, with Alfred the dog right behind.

Arthur's father reached the steps and sighed a deep sigh. His shirt was already beginning to dry. And, after all, it was only water. He tried to smile at his wife as she came up to join him, still a little clumsy without her glasses. She really was very endearing, he thought.

"I'm sorry, dear. I spoke harshly to you because I was startled," he said sincerely.

"Oh, no, it was my fault. Sometimes I am so clumsy," she confessed.

"No, no!" replied Arthur's father, who had been thinking the same thing. "Would you like some coffee?"

"I would love some," she answered, pleased by this little gesture of love.

Arthur's father took a cup, put in two lumps of sugar, and added a cloud of milk. While he did this, his wife was looking for her glasses in the various pockets of her dress. So she did not see the spider that was descending along a thread a few inches away from her face.

Arthur's father turned toward his wife, cup in one hand, coffeepot in the other, and began to pour the coffee delicately.

"A good cup of coffee will wake us up!" he commented.

He did not know how right he was. His wife had finally found her glasses and put them on. The first thing she saw was a monstrous spider, rubbing its hairy legs together, one inch from her nose.

She immediately let out a wild shriek. It sounded like a baboon having a fingernail ripped out. Her husband jumped back, tripped on the tray, and fell flat on the porch. The coffeepot flew out of his hands and emptied itself all over him. His cry, compared with hers, sounded more like a mammoth having a tooth pulled . . . so, whatever else you might think of them, at least the couple was harmonious in their pain.

CHAPTER
6

Their unworldly cry, times two, echoed to the ends of the Seven Lands and even beyond, as far as Necropolis.

Selenia looked up as if she could see the cry that had just passed, distorted, bouncing from wall to wall. Arthur finished sliding down the long spider thread and landed behind Selenia. He had also heard the sound, but he was light-years away from imagining that it could have come from his parents.

"Welcome to Necropolis," said the princess with a little smile.

"So far it is not as terrible as the welcome message was!" noted Arthur, who was already covered with cold sweat.

"Here, the word for welcome is the same as the word for death!" Selenia explained. "We have to stay together," she said just as Betameche arrived, knocking them down like bowling pins. The group scattered with a great deal of noise.

"Boy, you never miss an opportunity, do you?" groaned Selenia, climbing to her feet.

"I'm sorry," replied Betameche, beaming. He was delighted to be with them again.

Arthur got up and brushed himself off. He noticed with astonishment that the spider's thread was being pulled back up the hole. Selenia had seen it, too, but didn't seem worried.

"How will we get back if the spider isn't there?" asked Arthur.

"Who ever said we *would* get back?" replied the princess cynically. "We are on a mission here. Once it is done, then we'll have time to think about our return." With that, she started down another tunnel with a determined step, chin forward, as if she feared nothing and no one. Arthur and Beta followed without arguing.

The road they were taking soon led to another, this one as wide as a main street.

Our three heroes tried to be as inconspicuous and silent as possible, since this street, carved in the stone, was far from being deserted. There were peasants from all of the Seven Lands, there to sell their goods. There were gamouls loaded with carefully cut metal plaques and selenielle vendors who had come to dispose of their harvest.

Selenia slipped into the crowd headed toward the great market of Necropolis.

Arthur was amazed to see so many people and so many colors. He would never have suspected the existence of all this life only a few yards underground his grandmother's garden.

There was no comparison to the little village where he lived and its supermarket that he loved to visit.

This market was huge and full of life. It was the center of all commerce, all traffic. It was not the sort of place one went to unarmed, and Selenia kept her hand on the hilt of her sword. Mercenaries of all kinds strolled through the market, ready to sell their services. Street hawkers grabbed the last remaining free spaces. A few suspicious-looking types set up gambling tables in the middle of the road, where you could bet on anything, from a couple of raisins to a couple of camels. Impossible to know what you would win, but you could certainly lose your health.

Arthur was a little frightened by all this. He was certainly impressed by the mixture of happy commerce and disreputable behavior. It was an amazing coexistence that actually seemed to work. The reason was simple: the henchmen.

Above each street corner, at a reasonable height, was a sentry box with a henchman, surveying the joyous chaos. Surveillance was total and permanent. Calm reigned because M. the cursed ruled with the iron fist of terror.

The Necropolis market was the first thing that Maltazard created when he came to power. The prince of darkness became rich by filling the Seven Lands with hordes of henchmen that he had trained to pillage and steal on his behalf. But pillaging and stealing were not enough. He knew that much wealth remained hidden, buried, and even swallowed.

As soon as a henchmen attack was rumored, the villagers made their best treasures disappear. Not all of it, of course, since not finding anything would have angered the master, but enough that he could tell more was hidden away somewhere.

Maltazard killed very few citizens, but not because he was good-hearted. His mercy was purely commercial. "A person who dies is one less worker to build my palace," he loved to say.

The best way to extract the riches he could not steal was to encourage his people to spend them. The lure of gain, of wealth, the desire to possess . . . so Maltazard built, right into the rock, hundreds of galleries, where he offered stands at a good price. Maltazard, by all accounts, had a good head for business. This was how the Necropolis market began. Now it was enormous and it made a fortune for Maltazard, who received a commission on every item bought or sold, no matter how small.

Our friends advanced through the chaos with prudence and curiosity—prudence because of the henchmen standing above their heads at every crossroads, and curiosity, as they saw creatures of all kinds. Arthur had never even dreamed of beings this strange . . . like this odd group of animals with protruding eyes who were holding up their ears in order not to step on them.

"Who are they?" asked Arthur, very intrigued.

"The Balong-Botos. They are from the Third Land. They come here to be barbered," Betameche explained.

"Barbered?" Arthur said.

"Their fur is very highly valued, so they come to sell it in the market," Betameche explained. "It grows long enough to be shaved twice a year. That is how they make a living. The rest of the time, all they do is sleep."

"And why do they have such big ears?" Arthur wondered.

"The Balong-Botos do not kill animals, so they do not have fur coats from animal skins to protect themselves from the severe winters of their region. Instead, parents pull on the ears of their children, beginning when they are very young, so that they can lengthen enough for each Balong-Boto to roll itself up in them during the winter. That has been their tradition for thousands of years."

Arthur couldn't believe it. Like all kids his age, he hated having his ears pulled. It had never occurred to him that they could end up keeping him warm in winter.

Distracted by a baby Balong that was having its ears pulled, Arthur walked straight into a post. Two posts, to be exact. Arthur looked up and discovered that these two posts were legs attached to a rangy creature. It resembled a beanpole mounted on the legs of a pink flamingo.

"It's an Asparguetto," Beta noted in a low voice. "They are very big and very sensitive!"

"Do not take the trouble to excuse yourself, young man,"

said the animal, bending toward Arthur. On its face it had green plates for glasses, the color of candy, which looked almost like a mask. Underneath them, you could barely see its small blue eyes.

"I'm sorry! I didn't see you!" Arthur said politely.

"I am not transparent, you know!" the Asparguetto replied in a calm voice. "Not only do I have to bend all day to be able to move in this place that is so not designed for people my size, but then I have to suffer these constant insults to my person."

"I completely understand," said Arthur gently. "I used to be tall! I know what it's like!"

The Asparguetto looked at him blankly. "So it's not enough to bump into me—now you have decided to make fun of me?" asked the sensitive creature.

"No, no, not at all! I just meant that I used to be almost five feet tall and now I am only half an inch." Arthur knew he was digging himself in deeper. "I wanted to say that . . . it is not easy to be tall in the world of the small, but . . . it also not easy to be small in the world of the tall."

The creature did not know what to think about this. He peered down at the strange little short-legged fellow for a moment.

"You are excused," the Asparguetto finally said, closing the discussion. It went striding off over a few more stands on his way to another street.

"I warned you," said Betameche. "They are supersensitive!"

Arthur watched the Asparguetto disappear in a few long strides. Too amazed to respond, he turned back to Beta and encountered another rather strange group of animals in front of them. These were large, furry creatures, as round as balloons, with small weasel faces and a dozen legs in constant motion.

"Those are the Boulaguiris. They live in the forest of the Fifth Land," Betameche noted. "Their specialty is polishing pearls. If you bring them a pearl in bad condition, they will eat it and six months later, they will bring it back to you, more beautiful than ever."

Betameche had barely finished his description when a Boulaguiri proved his words. The creature approached a small stand carved into the stone. A Cachflot greeted him. The Cachflots were the only individuals authorized to run businesses in Necropolis. Whether buying or selling, all transactions passed through their hands. It was Maltazard himself who granted the privilege to this tribe from the far-off Sixth Land. Legend had it that their chief, named Cacarante, had saved the life of M. the cursed by lending him money so that he could have his face redone. The sovereign was not ungrateful, and he rewarded him in this way. The Cachflots had been growing rich in Necropolis for many years.

The Boulaguiri extended one of his paws to the vendor, who shook it civilly but without great enthusiasm. Politeness, here as elsewhere, is necessary for commerce.

After exchanging a few words that neither Arthur nor Betameche could hear, the Boulaguiri began to contort himself, as if he had been overcome with terrible stomach pains. Arthur grimaced in sympathy as if his own stomach felt just as bad.

The face of the Boulaguiri changed colors several times before shifting to the most sickening pale green color. Then he emitted a loud burp and a magnificent pearl popped out of his mouth. It fell into a box lined with black cotton that the Cachflot was holding. The dealer caught the pearl with a pair of tweezers, while the Boulaguiri slowly returned to his normal color.

The Cachflot examined the pearl. It was sublime, glowing with a thousand points of light. The buyer accepted the deal with a small nod of his head. The Boulaguiri gave him a beautiful smile, revealing that the creature did not have teeth. He began to contort himself for another delivery.

Arthur was amazed at this sight, even though such marvels were common in the streets leading to Necropolis. But a cry of joy awakened him from his reverie. Betameche had just found a seller of bellicornes. The boy was jumping for joy and began a little dance of thanks.

"What on earth is wrong with you?" asked Arthur.

Betameche grabbed his comrade by the shoulders. "These are bellicornes in syrup!" he shouted. "There is nothing better in all of the Seven Lands than bellicornes in syrup!"

"And what exactly are these bellicornes?" Arthur asked, wary of the culinary tastes of his friend.

"Dough made of sentinelle, soaked in gamoul's milk, then mixed with eggs to hold it together, sprinkled with chopped nuts, and covered with a delicious rosewater syrup." Betameche recited the recipe, savoring every word.

Arthur was delighted—there didn't appear to be anything weird about these cookies. They actually sounded a bit like gazelle horns, cookies his grandmother made from time to time using a recipe that she had brought back from Africa.

Betameche took a coin out of his pocket and threw it to the Cachflot, who caught it in midair.

"Serve yourself, my lord," he said, the perfect merchant.

Betameche took a bellicorne and bit into it. He let out a small sigh of satisfaction, then began to chew very slowly to make the pleasure last. Arthur could resist no longer. He took a bellicorne and bit off the end, shiny with syrup. He waited a few seconds, in case there were secondary effects, like there had been with the jack-fire, but nothing happened. The syrup melted in his mouth, while the lightly sweetened dough reminded him of almond paste. Arthur continued to eat.

"Isn't it the best thing that you have ever eaten in your entire life?" Betameche asked as he finished off his fourth bel-licorne.

Arthur had to admit that it was really good.

"Are my bellicornes really fresh?" asked the merchant, with

the smile of someone who already knows the answer.

The two friends nodded energetically, their mouths full of syrup.

"The rosewater came from this morning's roses and I picked the eggs myself barely an hour ago," he declared, a good baker proud of his product.

Arthur stopped dead in his tracks, his mouth wide open. One detail worried him. In his world, eggs were laid, they were collected, they were found, they were even stolen, but they were never "picked."

"Excuse me . . . what kind of eggs are they?" Arthur asked politely, making a face as if already expecting the worst. The vendor laughed at his client's naïveté.

"There is only one kind of egg suitable for making real bellicornes, of course. Caterpillar eggs, taken from underneath the mother," said the merchant. He proudly pointed to his official plaque, naming him one of the best bellicorne bakers of the year.

In response, Arthur spit out the contents of his mouth right into the man's face.

The vendor stood still for a moment, shocked by the insult that the young Arthur had accidentally made.

"I'm so sorry—I can't handle caterpillar or dragonfly eggs!" explained Arthur.

This was going to end badly, Beta could tell. He took advantage of the last few seconds of surprise to swallow a dozen cakes at a speed approaching the world record.

The Cachflot had regained his composure. He took a deep breath and began to shout: "Guards! Over here!"

At these simple words, there was panic in the street.

CHAPTER
7

Everyone ran around, yelling in various languages. Suddenly, a hand grabbed Arthur by the shoulder and pulled him violently back. "This way!" whispered Selenia as she dragged Arthur behind her. Betameche grabbed a few more bellicornes and joined his comrades, scattering cakes every which way.

The three heroes elbowed their way through the general panic, and ducked into a shop to avoid the patrol of henchmen that was rushing up the street.

Arthur caught his breath.

"We said to stay together, didn't we?" Selenia lectured them, annoyed at having to supervise two irresponsible boys.

"I know, but there were so many interesting people all of a sudden!" Arthur said.

"The more people you talk to, the more likely we are to be noticed. We have to be discreet!" Selenia insisted.

Another Cachflot, all smiles, appeared behind them. "Can't one be discreet and *elegant*, too?" he said in honeyed tones. "Come and take a look at my new collection. It's a feast for the eyes!"

As the merchant had guessed, no princess in the world could refuse this type of invitation.

Meanwhile, a little farther away, the bellicorne merchant was describing, with big, unflattering gestures, the two professional thieves who had assaulted him. The chief of the henchmen listened attentively. It did not take him long to realize that these must be the same runaways who had escaped from Darkos at the Jaimabar Club.

This type of news spreads quickly in Necropolis, because it is rare that inhabitants of the First Land come to visit the forbidden zones and even more rare for one of them to insult Prince Darkos.

The chief of the henchmen turned to his men.

"Search all the stores. They can't be far," he ordered.

Fortunately for our three heroes, the troops went off in the wrong direction.

The chief grabbed the last soldier by the neck. "You, go warn the palace." The soldier froze, and then took off like a rabbit.

Selenia saw him pass by their shop, faster than lightning.

"At least now we know the direction of the palace!" commented the princess. She threw a coin to the merchant, then buried her face in the hood of her new Balong-boto fur coat. Arthur and Betameche did the same. They looked like three penguins, disguised as Eskimos.

"My pleasure!" the smiling merchant called after them as they left.

The camouflage seemed effective—no one noticed them in their multicolored furs.

"You could have chosen something lighter. I am dying of the heat!" Betameche complained, buried in a fur that was too big for him. "We have to stop for something to drink," he added.

"You're hot, you're hungry, you're thirsty! When are you going to stop complaining all the time?" Selenia asked in utter exasperation.

Betameche scowled and began to grumble quietly to himself.

Selenia picked up the pace, afraid of losing track of the henchman. The street became slightly wider, then opened onto an enormous square, located in a cave whose roof was so high it could not be seen from the ground.

Selenia stopped at the edge of this monumental arena, where thousands of onlookers were milling around.

"The Necropolis market," whispered Selenia, awed by the size of the place. She had heard it described many times, but everything that she had imagined was smaller than this. The square was filled with people, and the crowds moved like the surface of an agitated sea. Things were bought, sold, exchanged, discussed, argued over, stolen. . . .

Arthur was speechless before this spectacle. One pair of eyes was not enough to take in the multitude of sights. It reminded him of his grandpa's enormous bait bucket, filled with hundreds of worms. The vision before him was just as colorful and certainly noisier.

They could hardly hear over the roar and babble, and Selenia had to yell to be heard. "I've lost sight of him," she shouted, annoyed. It was not surprising that the henchman had disappeared, given the chaos in the market.

"Why don't we just ask the way to the palace? People here must know where it is, right?" asked Arthur naively.

"You don't understand. Everything is sold here, and it is information that sells the best. Ask for the palace and you will be handed over to the guards in a minute!" said Selenia.

Arthur looked around him and noticed that no one looked very trustworthy at all. They all had bulging eyes, jaws full of teeth, furs that were too long, and legs that were too numerous. He had never seen such a variety of weapons as those hanging from every belt. It was like a real western.

Our three heroes craned their heads in all directions, searching the crowd for a sign that might put them on the path to the palace.

On the other side of the square was a monumental façade, sculpted with all kinds of strange faces. It looked more like the entrance to a horror museum than a palace but, knowing the personality of M. the cursed, Selenia felt she was on the right path.

Working their way through this crowd, which was thicker than the thickest pea soup, took them about twenty minutes. Finally they arrived at the foot of the façade.

"Do you think this is it?" whispered Betameche. "It seems kind of scary for a palace!"

"Given the number of guards in front of the door, I'm guessing it's not the entrance to a kindergarten!" Selenia replied.

Actually, in front of the imposing door, which was locked three times, were two full rows of menacing henchmen, each of whom looked ready to slice up anyone who dared to approach, even to ask for directions.

"Maybe there's a back entrance," Selenia suggested.

"Good idea," her two followers replied in unison, not really in the mood to take on two rows of henchmen.

Suddenly, the crowd behind them opened up to let a procession pass.

"Room! Room," cried a potbellied henchman. He was leading a convoy consisting of a dozen wagons piled high with fruit, grilled insects, and other equally delicious dishes. They were all pulled by gamouls, who were somewhat jumpy in the midst of such a large crowd.

Selenia approached to watch the convoy pass. "What's going

on?" she casually asked a stranger with bulging eyes.

"It's the master's meal. The fifth of the day!" noted the stranger, who was as thin as a rail.

"And how many does he have like this?" asked Betameche, slightly envious.

"Eight meals a day, like the fingers of his hands," answered the old man with the hungry face, watching the convoy pass by.

"And he's going to eat all that?" wondered Arthur.

"What do you think? He barely touches it. All he eats is a grilled insect or two. When I think that one of these meals could nourish my people for six moons!" the old man confessed. He sighed with despair and moved on, disgusted by this opulence.

"Why doesn't M. give away the food that he doesn't eat rather than throwing it out?" said Arthur.

"M. the cursed is evil personified. He takes pleasure in the suffering he inflicts on others. Nothing gives him more pleasure than a starving people crying for their survival," explained Selenia through clenched teeth.

"But he was one of you once, wasn't he?" Arthur asked.

"Who told you that?" asked the princess, visibly disturbed by the question.

"Beta told me that he was chased from your land a long time ago," the boy replied.

Selenia gave her brother an angry look that he carefully

avoided by looking elsewhere. "It's crazy, all these little details on the palace façade, isn't it?" Beta said, trying to change the subject.

"What happened? Why was he chased away?" asked Arthur. He'd forgotten his decision not to ask any more questions—he was dying to know a little bit more about the Minimoys and this terrible enemy.

"It's a long story that I'll tell you later. Perhaps! In the meantime, we have better things to do. Follow me!" Selenia elbowed through the hungry crowd and started walking along next to the convoy.

A little creature called a sylo was watching the food pass, his eight big eyes wide open. Hungrily, he reached out toward a piece of fruit. A violent crack of the whip hit his hand and he yelped.

The parents of the little sylo immediately hid him in their thick fur. A henchman stopped in front of the father sylo, his whip in his hands.

"We do not touch the master's food," the henchman reminded them.

The sylo bared its teeth, forty-eight razor-sharp blades. One more move against his child would probably have been very dangerous.

The henchman swallowed upon seeing this chain saw.

"All right, we'll let it go—this time," the henchman conceded.

Next to the enormous palace entrance, there was a cave cut into the rock wall. At the back of the cave was another, smaller heavy door, modestly decorated. As the convoy approached, this swung open automatically. The procession entered slowly, wagon after wagon rolling into the heart of the rock.

The crowd stood back from this entrance. No one dared to go any closer. No one, that is, except for our three heroes. Selenia had hidden herself behind a large rock nearby and was watching for the last wagon to pass through. She threw off her fur coat and prepared to jump.

"This is where our paths separate, Arthur," said the princess.

"No way!" replied the valiant Arthur. "I'm coming with you!"

But Selenia unsheathed her sword, faster than lightning, and pointed it at his throat to keep him away.

"This is something I have to do myself," said Selenia gravely.

"And me? What do I do?" asked the boy.

"You find the treasure and save your home. I will find M. the cursed and try to save mine," Selenia said in a low, determined voice. "If I succeed, we will meet back here in an hour," she added solemnly.

"And if you fail?" asked Arthur, sadness gripping him.

Selenia let out a long sigh. She had considered this possibility many times. She knew that her chances were very slim against M. the cursed and his infinite powers.

She had perhaps one chance in a thousand to succeed, but she was a real princess of the blood, daughter of King Sifrat de Matradoy, fifteenth of that name. There was no question that she would fight to the finish, no matter what.

She looked into Arthur's eyes and approached him, without lowering her sword.

"If I fail ... be a good king," she said simply, as if a little door had just opened in her soldier's heart. She put her hand on his shoulder and placed a gentle kiss on his mouth.

Time stood still. Bees drew hearts with honey in a sky where carnations rained down. The clouds held hands around them, and an orchestra of thousands of birds drowned the sky with beautiful melody.

Never had Arthur felt so happy. He felt like he was sliding on a silk toboggan through the air. Selenia's breath was warmer than summer, her skin softer than springtime. He wouldn't have minded staying there for centuries, if the gods of love had let him.

Selenia stepped back and broke the charm.

The kiss had lasted only a second.

Selenia smiled at him. Her look had a new sweetness. "Now that you have all my powers ... make good use of them." She turned and leaped for the door, darting through the gap just before it clanged shut.

"But—wait ... we must ..." murmured Arthur, starting after

her. But even though Arthur was only half an inch tall, there was no way for him to slip in. The door was shut. Selenia was gone.

Arthur was overwhelmed. He had barely had time to understand what was happening to him and already he had to understand that it might never happen again. The young man touched his lips, as if to reassure himself that he had not been dreaming, but the princess's perfume was still there, all around his face.

Betameche came out from his hiding place, applauding. "Bravo! That was wonderful!" He grabbed Arthur's hands and shook them vigorously. "Congratulations! That was one of the most beautiful weddings I have ever attended!"

"What are you talking about?" asked Arthur, somewhat lost.

"Why, about your marriage, idiot! She kissed you. So you are married, for better or for worse, until the next dynasty. That's how it is with us!" Beta explained simply.

"You mean to tell me that—that kiss, that was marriage?" questioned Arthur, somewhat surprised by this bizarre custom.

"Of course!" confirmed Betameche. "A very moving ceremony! Clear! Concise! Superb!"

"A little *too* concise, wasn't it?" asked Arthur, disoriented by the speed of events.

"Of course not! You have the main parts: her hand and her heart. What more could you want?" Betameche retorted with a logic belonging only to the Minimoys.

"Where I live, adults take a little more time. They get to know each other, they go out with each other, spend time together. Then they discuss it, and it is usually the man who makes the proposal. Then the kiss comes at the end, after they say 'I do!' in front of a minister and a whole lot of people," Arthur explained, thinking of his parents' marriage.

"Oh, my! What a waste of time! You must have a lot of time to spare if you spend so much of it on little details. It's only the head that needs all of this artifice. The heart understands the truth of things, and a kiss is the best way to say it," said Betameche.

Everything was moving much too fast for Arthur. After a kiss like that, he needed a good night's sleep and some aspirin.

"What more did you want?" his friend asked, seeing his crestfallen expression.

"Well . . . I don't know. A little celebration, perhaps?" said Arthur.

"That sounds like an excellent idea to me," said a voice too deep to be Beta's.

Our two friends turned around and found themselves face-to-face with twenty henchmen. They were all grouped behind their chief, the horrible Darkos, only son of the equally horrible M. the cursed.

Each time Darkos smiled, he looked as if he were going

to kill someone, his smile was so unfriendly. Even if he'd brushed his brown teeth fifteen times a day, it would change nothing.

Darkos approached Arthur with the slow step of a conqueror. "I will personally take care of preparing a small celebration," he said. The message was so clear that even the henchmen understood it and laughed stupidly.

Arthur also understood. This was going to be much less pleasant than his birthday party a few short days ago.

Arthur's mother was sitting at the kitchen table. She fingered the ten little candles that no longer had a cake or Arthur to shine for.

Ten little candles, for ten short years that had seen Arthur shoot up like a young wild animal. Arthur's poor mother could not stop remembering those ten birthdays, all of them different.

The first, when the light of the candles dancing in front of him had enchanted Arthur. The second, when he tried, in vain, to catch the little flames that slipped between his hands. The third birthday, when his still small breath required three tries to blow out all the candles. The fourth cake when he blew the candles out all together for the first time. The fifth, when he cut the cake himself, under the vigilant eye of his father, helping him handle a knife that was too big for his hand. The sixth birthday, the most important in Arthur's eyes, because on this occasion his grandfather had given him his own knife with which he proudly cut his own cake. It was also the last birthday his grandfather was there for.

The poor woman could not prevent a tear from rolling down her cheek. There had been so much happiness and unhappiness in only ten years. Next to these ten years that had flashed by like a shooting star, the ten hours that had passed since she found out about Arthur's disappearance seemed like an eternity.

Arthur's mother looked around for something to comfort her, something that would give her a bit of hope. All she saw was her husband, stretched out on the couch, overcome by fatigue. He didn't have the strength to snore or even to close his mouth, which was open to the four winds.

Under other circumstances, this picture would have made her smile, but today, it made her want to cry even more.

Grandma sat down next to her with a box of tissues.

"That's my last box," she said with sad humor.

The daughter looked at her mother and sighed a small sigh.

In difficult moments, the old woman had always been able to keep her sense of humor. She got that from her husband, Archibald, who elevated humor and poetry to the rank of basic values.

"Humor is to life what cathedrals are to religion—it is the best that we have invented," he liked to joke.

If only Archibald were here, Grandma thought. He would bring a bit of light into their now dark lives. He would know how to give them that little touch of optimism that never left him and that enabled him to make it through the war, the way a matador escapes the horns of a bull.

The old woman gently grasped her daughter's hands and shook them with affection. "You know, my dear daughter . . . what I am going to say probably makes no sense, but . . . your son is an exceptional little boy. Wherever he is, even if he finds himself in a bad situation, I have a feeling he will be able to get out of it."

Arthur's mother seemed somewhat reassured by these words, and the two women held each other's hands as if preparing to pray.

They would have to hope that Grandma was right because, for the moment, Arthur was in prison. His two little hands held the iron bars, and he watched the marketplace full of people, where there was not a single kind soul to come to his aid.

"Forget it! No one would risk helping a prisoner of M. the cursed," said Beta, huddling in a corner in the prison.

"Watch what you say, Beta! Selenia said we had to be careful," Arthur reminded him.

"Careful? Everyone already knows we are in prison!" sighed the little prince, completely depressed. "We have fallen into the hands of this monster. Our future is already clear! Only Selenia can save our lives . . . provided, of course, that she can save her own!"

Arthur looked at him and was forced to agree. Selenia was their only hope.

CHAPTER
8

Our little princess was advancing through the maze of unwelcoming halls in
the royal palace, her hands firmly gripping her sword. She lost
sight of the food convoy but managed to orient herself by the
tracks left on the ground by the wooden wheels. She moved
quietly from hiding place to hiding place, regularly allowing
patrols of henchmen, which were as numerous as frogs in a
pond, to pass.

Soon, the corridors dug into the rock became increasingly
more ornate and the walls were covered with black marble.
Flames from the torches were reflected in the smooth surface,
making the hall appear endless.

Selenia's heart was beating regularly, but her hands were a
little damp. This icy underground world was not exactly her
favorite place to be. She preferred forests of tall grass, autumn
leaves that made it possible to surf the hills of her village, fields
of poppies in which it was so comfortable to sleep. A wave of
homesickness swept over her. It is often only when we are

experiencing unhappiness that we realize how valuable little day-to-day things really are: a great stretch upon waking, a ray of sunlight on your face, someone you love smiling at you. It's as if unhappiness is simply a way to measure happiness.

A patrol of henchmen brought Selenia back from her reverie, making her jump into a nearby doorway to hide from them.

She could not think of home now; she had to focus on her mission. She was still inside this palace of death, a black cathedral, as cold as ice. The floor was also marble, and of such a deep black that it created the illusion of falling. The tracks of the wagons were no longer visible. This stone was too hard to have any trace left on it.

Selenia arrived at a crossroads and had to make a decision. She stood there for a moment, relying on her instincts to guide her. Was there a force watching over these Seven Lands that would lend a hand, or would she have to face this test on her own?

Selenia waited a little, but no divine sign appeared. Not even a slight breeze to indicate the road to choose. She sighed and once again examined the two tunnels. There was a vague light in the one on the right and what sounded like distant music. A normal person would have immediately sensed danger and fled in the other direction. But Selenia was not a normal person. She was a princess devoted to her cause and ready to take any risk to accomplish her mission. She grasped the sword in her hand harder and entered the passageway on the right.

Soon she came to a corner and found herself in an enormous room. Dark slabs of glowing marble covered the ground, while thousands of stalactites hung from the ceiling, drops of water frozen in their descent.

Selenia took a few steps on the marble, as smooth as a lake, which seemed to absorb all sound. At the back of the room, she saw the wagons left by the slaves. Fruits of all kinds were overflowing the cart, the only traces of color in this universe of gray and black.

In front of the cart was a silhouette, its back turned to Selenia. She could see it was wearing a long cape, ragged at the ends, placed over asymmetrical shoulders. It was difficult, from this distance, to say whether the man wore a hat or whether his head was just a lot bigger than his body. It didn't matter— this emaciated silhouette was monstrous and seemed to come straight out of our worst nightmares.

This man with his back turned, nibbling bits of fruit from the ends of his clawlike fingers, could be no one but M. the cursed.

Selenia swallowed, grasped her sword to give herself courage, and advanced with slow, muffled steps.

Her vengeance was within reach. It was her own personal revenge but also that of all her people and all the peoples of the Seven Lands who, at one time or another, had been subject to the warlike arm of this conquering emperor.

Selenia's arm would correct all that and cleanse the memory

of the ancestors, soiled by years of slavery and dishonor. Her eyes riveted on her enemy, she advanced slowly, her breath short, her heart pounding. She raised her arm slowly in the air.

Unfortunately, the sword was long and the stalactites here were much lower than the others. As she lifted it, the blade struck the stone with a small, shrill sound.

The silhouette, holding a piece of fruit, froze in place. Selenia did likewise. She was as immobile as the rocks hanging from the ceiling.

The man set the fruit down carefully and let out a long, calm sigh. He still had his back to Selenia. He lifted his head, as if overwhelmed but not surprised by her presence.

"I once spent entire days polishing that sword, so that its blade would be perfect. I would recognize the sound it makes among a thousand others." The man's voice was cavernous. The walls of his throat must have been badly damaged because the air that passed through blew strangely, as if it were in contact with a cheese grater.

"It was not you," the man mused. "So who, then, was able to pull this sword from the stone, Selenia?" he asked, before slowly turning around.

Maltazard finally showed his face and it was a walking horror. Deformed, half eaten away, wrinkled by time, his face was nothing more than a devastated field. Crusts had formed here and there around still-weeping wounds. The pain must be constant and it showed in his worn-out expression.

You might have expected to see nothing there but fire and hatred. Quite the contrary; his eyes had the sadness of animals on the path to extinction, the melancholy of fallen princes, and the humility of survivors.

But Selenia did not gaze too deeply into the eyes of Maltazard. She knew they were the most formidable of his weapons. How many had fallen into the trap of his harmless look and ended up being toasted like almonds?

She held her sword in front of her, prepared for an evil blow, observing Maltazard and the rest of his body. It did not seem like much. Half Minimoy, half insect, it seemed to be decomposing. Some coarse stitching held most of him together and his long cape hid the rest as best it could.

His jaws opened slightly. This might have been a smile, or at least an attempt at one.

"I am very happy to see you, princess," he said in a softer voice. "I missed you," he added, apparently sincere.

Selenia stood straight and lifted her chin, like the courageous young woman she had become.

"I didn't miss you," she replied. "And I am here to destroy you!"

Clint Eastwood could not have done better. She fixed her gaze on Maltazard, ready for a duel, as if totally unaware of the impressive size of her adversary. It was David against Goliath, Mowgli against Shere Khan.

"Why so much hatred?" asked Maltazard, smiling even more at the idea of combat.

"You betrayed your people and massacred or enslaved all the others. You are a monster!"

"Don't speak of monsters," said Maltazard, whose face had turned green. "Don't speak of things you don't understand," he added, calming himself down. "If you knew how painful it is to live in this mutilated body, you would not say such things."

"Your body was in perfect condition when you betrayed us. It was the gods that inflicted this punishment on you!" retorted the princess, determined not to give in on any point.

Maltazard let out a thunderous roar, like a cannon spitting out a cannonball.

"My poor child—if only history could be that simple, or if only I had been able to forget . . ." he admitted with a sigh. "At one time I was known as Maltazard the good, Maltazard the warrior! He who watches and protects," he added with tears in his voice as he went on to tell his story.

Once Maltazard had been a handsome Minimoy, strong and smiling. He stood three heads taller than anyone else, which resulted in teasing by his comrades. "His parents must have given him too much gamoul's milk!" they amused themselves by saying. It made him smile. He did not have much of a sense of humor, but he knew that these little jokes were compliments in disguise. Everyone admired his strength and his courage.

After the death of his parents, casualties in the war with the Sauterelles—a war that pitted the two peoples against each other for many moons—no one dared to utter even the mildest of jokes about him anymore.

Maltazard became an adult without the pain of his parents' loss ever leaving his heart. True to the principles that his parents had taught him, he was courageous and obliging. His sense of honor and country were deeply developed.

When the terrible drought began that would last almost a thousand Minimoy years, an expedition was sent out to search for water. Even though the Minimoys do not like to get wet, water was necessary for agriculture and for the survival of the Minimoy people.

It was natural that Maltazard would ask permission to lead the expedition. The king, still young at the time, gave him the command with great pleasure. Maltazard was like the son he wanted to have—the kind of son that the king hoped Betameche would become one day. But in the meantime, the little prince was only a few weeks old, and the king placed all his hopes in Maltazard.

Selenia fought like a tigress, since she believed *she* should be in charge of this important mission. Even though she was still young, and no taller than a raisin, she said that only a princess of the blood was worthy of this mission. The king had a very difficult time calming her down and had to promise her that she would one day get her turn to serve her people.

So, one fine morning Maltazard set out, as proud as a conqueror, his chest filled with ardor and courage. He left the village to the sound of applause and cries of encouragement. Several young women could not stop their tears when they saw their national hero pass by, on the road to glory.

After a few days, the expedition took a turn for the worse. The drought had reached all the lands. The survivors had organized themselves into bands, and they protected their goods fiercely. Maltazard and his men were attacked by looters both day and night, falling from the trees, emerging from the mud or even the air.

After only one month of travel, only half of the wagons were left, and only a third of the men were alive to drive them.

The deeper they went into the interior of the lands, the more they encountered hostile territories, populated by ferocious beasts that until then had been unknown to them. The forests were filled with bloody hordes that were only interested in drinking and plundering, usually at the same time.

Each stream or natural well that they discovered was already desperately dry. They had to push on, farther and farther. The expedition traveled through carnivorous forests; lakes of dried mud; then barren, contaminated plateaus that civilization seemed to have abandoned.

Maltazard experienced all this suffering, all this humiliation, without batting an eye. He would never fail in his mission, and when, in the middle of a mountain, almost impenetrable, he finally found a small freshwater stream, he was not surprised.

Unfortunately, all that remained of the glorious expedition were four soldiers and one wagon to protect it. Maltazard and his men filled the water tank to the brim and started on their way back.

The return trip was a horror.

No more beautiful principles, rules of art, chivalry. Maltazard protected the water for his people the way a starving dog protects its bone. Each day he became more monstrous, not hesitating to cut in half anyone who represented a threat, and he passed from the art of defense to the art of attack.

It was, he said, the best way to anticipate problems. A good attack, rapid and bloody, would avoid any discussion and save the trouble of mounting a defense afterward.

Maltazard became, without realizing it, an enraged animal without any limits, blinded by his mission. His last soldiers died in bloody combat, and he finished the voyage alone, pulling with his bare hands the cistern that contained the precious liquid.

He arrived at the village at sunrise. He was welcomed with incredible acclaim—a welcome that is reserved only for true heroes, those who walk on the Moon or save entire countries with shots of vaccine.

As a savior, Maltazard was carried through the village on the shoulders of the people.

When he arrived before the king, he had just enough energy to tell him that the mission was accomplished, before collapsing, unconscious, worn out.

Selenia watched Maltazard as he told his story. She was interested but did not let any emotion show on her face. She knew the powers of this magician who could manipulate words as well as weapons.

"A few months later, the illness and evil spells contracted during the trip began to change my body," Maltazard continued in a voice full of emotion. "The rest of the story is the most tragic and the most painful to tell.

"Little by little, fear invaded the village. It was the fear of being contaminated. People moved away when I passed. No one spoke to me, or spoke very little. Smiles were polite but forced. The more my body deteriorated, the more people tried to avoid me. I ended up alone in my hut, cut off from the rest of the world, alone with my pain that no one wanted to share. I, Maltazard the hero, savior of the village, I had become, in just a few months, Maltazard . . . the cursed! Until the day they decided not even to pronounce my name and to call me by a letter: M. . . . the cursed!"

The fallen hero stopped, as if overwhelmed by so many painful memories.

Selenia waited several seconds. It was not her way to make

fun of the suffering of others, but it was her intention, calmly, to tell the truth.

"The version in the history book is somewhat different," she finally said.

Maltazard perked up, intrigued. He clearly did not know that his little story was included in the great Minimoy history book.

"And . . . what does the official version say?" Maltazard asked curiously.

The princess assumed her most neutral voice and recited what she had learned at school. At the time, her professor of history had been Miro the mole. Who, better than he, at fifteen thousand years of age, could recite the Great History? Selenia adored the classes when Miro got carried away, reliving the great battles, shedding a tear at the memory of marriages and coronations that he had had the honor of organizing. Each time he told about the great invasions, he could not stop himself from climbing on the tables, enacting the stories of heroes attacked from all sides, fighting alone against the enemy.

He always ended his classes exhausted and left immediately for a good nap. He knew the story of Maltazard by heart, and it was probably the only one that he told calmly, with much respect.

It was true Maltazard had left as a hero, with the king's blessing. The expedition lasted several months and was really terrible. The great warrior, who had learned to fight with honor and respect, very quickly had had to learn new ways to stay alive.

The external world, weakened by drought, had become an inferno in which, in order to survive, it was necessary to do evil things. Stories from far-off lands were carried back by traveling peddlers or lost travelers, and the Minimoy people were able to follow from a distance the fall of their hero who, tired of the constant attacks, began to plunder in turn. He may have fought for a noble cause and the survival of his people, but he looted and massacred to achieve his ends.

This made everyone back home uneasy. The great council met and debated for ten moons. When they finished, exhausted, they had a new text, which was called *The Great Book of Ideas*.

The Great Book of Ideas served as the basis for a major reorganization of the Minimoy world. The king wanted a more just society, based on respect for people and all things.

In a few weeks, the village was transformed. Nothing was cut down or torn without careful thought. Nothing was thrown away. Everyone joined together to learn how to recover and reuse everything. This was the third commandment. It was an idea that Archibald the benevolent had expressed years before and that they had never forgotten.

"Nothing is ever lost, nothing is ever created, everything is transformed." He admitted that the idea was not his originally, but that was of no importance.

The second commandment was taken from a book that Archibald also often spoke of, but that had a title no one could remember. "Love and respect your neighbor as yourself." This commandment was highly valued and everyone kept it well. People smiled more; they greeted each other; and they invited each other to share meals, even when the drought made it difficult.

The first commandment was by far the most important and had been inspired by Maltazard's misadventure: "Nothing justifies the death of an innocent." The council had adopted this idea without discussion and unanimously chose it to be the first commandment.

There were three hundred sixty-five commandments in all, treasured by those worthy to call themselves Minimoys.

While Maltazard had cruelly changed during his trip, Minimoy society had also followed a difficult path. When Maltazard returned to his village—not alone, as he claimed, but with his wagon pulled by a dozen slaves that he had captured en route—he received a mixed welcome.

Of course, the king thanked him for the lifesaving water, but there was no great celebration, as he had hoped.

First the slaves were freed and given food to last for several days as they journeyed back to their homes. Then there were many prayers for the Minimoys who had not returned from the expedition. Maltazard was the only survivor. He was the only one who could tell how his troops had been decimated, and many Minimoys had doubts about the exact details of these deaths.

But Maltazard did not notice their suspicions, and he took great pleasure in narrating his exploits. He described his journey in great detail, emphasizing his bravery and his courage, which got bigger and more impressive each time he told the story.

People listened politely, according to the eighth commandment that gives each individual the right to express himself and commandment number two hundred forty-seven, which states that it is impolite to cut somebody off.

But very soon the exploits of Maltazard the glorious ceased to interest people.

Maltazard found himself more and more alone—confronted with himself, struggling with his past.

Miro advised him to read *The Great Book of Ideas*, but Maltazard would hear nothing of it, let alone read it. He did not understand how they could have written such a book without waiting for his advice.

He had traveled through the Seven Lands—up, down, and across. He had battled the most fearsome people, survived indescribable storms, defeated animals that even a crazed imagination could not invent. None of this experience had been taken into consideration for the *Great Book* and Maltazard was extremely angry about it.

"It was not a guide to warfare that we were trying to write

but a guide to good behavior!" Miro told him. This response put Maltazard in a black rage. He left the village and began to get drunk in neighboring bars, reciting his tales of war to anyone who would listen.

Every day, he buried himself deeper in bad living, consorting with the worst insects, often poisonous, including one rather pretty young coleopteron who . . .

"Be quiet!" Maltazard suddenly cried.

Selenia smiled at him. Judging by the beads of sweat on Maltazard's forehead, there was a good chance that her version of the story was much closer to the truth than Maltazard's.

"I met that young woman for only a second," he defended himself, sounding very guilty.

"You gave her your powers and she gave you hers!" replied the princess sharply.

"That's enough!" screamed Maltazard, mad with rage. Such fury was not good for him, since, as soon as he became angry, the wounds on his face oozed open, smelling horrible, as if the pressure that was inside had to find a way out.

Selenia was not impressed, but she was moved by the pain that she could read in Maltazard's face. While he did not like to be contradicted, he liked it less when he was looked straight in the eye, and still less when it was with compassion.

He turned around and began to walk back into his immense marble salon.

"I did celebrate my victories in several neighboring bars,

People were so interested in my exploits that it would have been cruel to deprive them of a chance to hear them!"

"There, you see!" muttered Selenia between her teeth.

"And one memorable evening I met a remarkable individual, from a very good family," Maltazard went on.

"A coleopteris venemis, pretty to look at but dangerous to be with!" Selenia specified.

"I know! I know!" Maltazard replied, annoyed by Selenia's common sense. "I let myself go, carried away by memories. She had me wrapped around her little finger. She drank in my words. And in the night, in colors of the shadowy half-light, she probably stole a kiss . . ." he admitted with some sadness. "A poisonous kiss. In the days that followed, I began to decompose, eaten away by the poison that attacked my body. That is how a single kiss ruined my entire life."

"A single kiss is enough to bind you to someone for life. As a Minimoy you should have remembered that," Selenia reminded him, but Maltazard was no longer listening. He was overcome with nostalgia and sadness.

"I left the village in search of healers capable of stopping this evil spell. I was a guinea pig for all kinds of potions. They made me eat all kinds of disgusting dishes, covered with the most repulsive creams. I even had to eat worms, raised to feed on this poison. They all died before even reaching my stomach. In the Fifth Land, I encountered several wizards who took a lot of my money in exchange for ridiculous charms. I ate every kind of root that can be found in the kingdom, but nothing could ease my pain. A life completely ruined because of a simple kiss."

Maltazard sighed, overcome by the sadness of his life.

"Next time, be more careful in choosing a partner," Selenia said.

Maltazard gave her a dark look. "You are right, Selenia," he said, pulling himself together. "Next time I will choose the most beautiful partner—one like a magnificent flower, one that I have seen grow and that I have always dreamed of picking."

Maltazard smiled and Selenia began to worry.

"A healing tree told me the secret that will free me of this sickness that devours me."

"Trees always give good advice," admitted Selenia, instinctively taking a step back.

It didn't matter because Maltazard, without even being aware of it, had taken one toward her.

"Only the powers of a royal flower, young and pure, can free me from the spell and restore my Minimoy appearance. A single kiss from this flower and I will be cured!"

Maltazard was slowly advancing.

"The kiss of a princess has power only if it is unique!" replied Selenia, who knew a lot about this subject.

"I know, but if my information is correct . . . you are not yet married," he said confidently, only too happy to see his trap snap shut.

"Your information is somewhat out of date," she said.

Maltazard stiffened. If this news was true, it was a catastrophe, condemning him to spend the rest of his life in this miserable carcass.

There was a little cough from the doorway, and Darkos entered the room.

It would have to be a real emergency for him to disregard protocol, which normally required him to be announced and to wait until his father deigned to see him.

Maltazard signaled for him to approach with a slight nod of his head, sensing that this visit must be of the utmost importance.

Darkos approached his father with care—he never knew what Maltazard was capable of doing—and murmured several words in his ear.

Maltazard's eyes widened to twice their size. It was true. The princess had married . . . without any announcement, without even sending out invitations.

Maltazard was shocked. Any hope for a return to his normal life had vanished—just like that—in a few seconds, with this confirmation. He was groggy for a few moments, like a boxer surprised by a left hook. His knees weakened and he swayed in place, but soon he regained control of himself.

For so long, he had held on to hope, being patient. He had absorbed more blows in his life than a punching bag. Now he let out a sigh, suffering this latest bitter and irrevocable defeat.

"Well played," he told the princess, who was watching him warily. "You are more intelligent than I thought. In order not to succumb to my charms, you offered your heart to the first person who came along."

"It was actually the last one," she replied with a bit of humor.

Maltazard turned his back to her and slowly approached the cart filled with fruit.

"You have given this young child an inestimable gift, the value of which he himself is unaware, and so he will do nothing," he said. "You had the power to save my life and you didn't. Don't count on me to save yours."

He seized an enormous raisin. "And to make you understand what my suffering has been like, you are going to suffer, too, before dying," he added, with a touch of true cruelty. "You will watch as your people are exterminated in the most horrible pain."

Selenia's blood ran cold.

Maltazard looked at his raisin, as if he had already moved on to something else. Or perhaps he was imagining that the fruit was one of his innocent victims.

A tear ran down Selenia's cheek. A burst of heat, of hatred, was rising inside her and she could do nothing to stop it. She seized her sword, lifted her vengeful arm, and threw the blade with all her might. The sword cut through the air like a bolt of lightning and sliced right through Maltazard. Unfortunately, the cursed prince was so eaten away by poison that his body was mostly holes, and the sword ended up flying through one of these and nailing the raisin to the cart. Maltazard looked at the sword that had passed through his body without even touching it.

For once my mutilated body has been good for something! he thought, amazed to see how destiny was playing with his life. He who, only a few minutes before, had cursed this body, was now glad to still have it.

He regarded the red juice that flowed from the fruit and put his finger under it to collect a few drops.

"I will drink the blood of your people as I drink that of this fruit," he said evilly.

At these words, Selenia no longer heard her fear but only her heart, which was racing furiously.

She ran toward Maltazard . . . but she was too late. Henchmen were pouring in from everywhere and surrounding Darkos, who had placed himself in front of his father to protect him.

The guards grabbed Selenia. It was impossible to escape from these mountains of steel and muscle. The princess was lost and disarmed.

Maltazard pulled the sword from the wood and turned toward Selenia. He looked delighted for a moment at her helplessness.

"Have no regrets, Selenia," he said slyly. "Even if you had married me, I should tell you . . . I would have exterminated your people just the same!"

Selenia burst into tears. "You are a monster, Maltazard!" she sobbed.

The prince of darkness smiled grimly. He had heard this insult so many times.

"I know. I get that from my first wife," he answered, his humor as black as his look. "Take her away!"

CHAPTER
9

Arthur was on his knees in front of the prison bars. He had exhausted himself shaking them.

"I am barely married and I already have the feeling that I am a widower. A widower and a prisoner," he noted, sick to his stomach.

This thought was enough to give him a bit more courage. He got up and began to shake the bars for the millionth time. Nothing happened, of course. Prison bars are made to resist all kinds of assaults.

"We have to get out of here, Beta! We have to come up with something," he cried.

"I'm thinking, Arthur, I'm thinking!" Betameche assured him. The Minimoy prince was comfortably curled up on a minuscule bed of grass. He seemed more in search of sleep than anything else.

"How can you sleep at a time like this?" said Arthur angrily.

"I'm not sleeping!" the little prince responded grouchily.

"I am pulling together all the energy that I normally use for walking, talking, and eating, and I am reorganizing it . . . into a single force . . . in order to . . . better be able . . ."

"To fall asleep!" Arthur concluded, as he watched his friend slowly nod off.

"That's it . . ." answered Betameche, who was finally asleep. Arthur kicked him in the shins, which was almost as effective as a cold shower. Betameche was on his feet in a second.

Arthur grabbed his shoulders.

"Beta, the powers! The powers Selenia gave me when she kissed me?" he said.

"Yes, a very nice kiss, very sweet," commented Betameche.

"What exactly are these powers?" Arthur persisted.

"Oh, that!" the prince answered. "I don't know."

"What do you mean you don't know?"

"She is the only one who knows what she has given you," Betameche replied, as if it were obvious.

Arthur was crestfallen. "That's fantastic. She gives me powers, in case I have to use them, but then she doesn't tell me what they are. Your tribe has a very strange idea of sharing!" Arthur grumbled.

"That's not exactly the way it works among us," Betameche replied maliciously. "Normally when you marry someone, it's because you know her and appreciate her gifts. When the marriage takes place, she doesn't need to tell you what she has to offer. You already know it."

"But I have only known her for two days!" cried Arthur, completely infuriated.

"Yes, but you still married her, didn't you?" replied her younger brother.

"A sword was being held to my throat!" Arthur defended himself.

"Oh? Do you mean that if you didn't have a sword at your throat you wouldn't have married her?"

"Of course I would have!" Arthur replied angrily.

"And you did! It was a beautiful wedding!" concluded Betameche with his own mysterious logic.

Arthur looked at him the way a chicken would look at a remote control. He felt a bit like an old knight battling windmills. He didn't think his nerves would be able to stand it much longer.

"Yes, it was a beautiful wedding. And I promise you a beautiful funeral if you don't help me to get out of here," he cried, going for Beta's throat.

"Stop! You're strangling me!" Betameche yelled.

"I know I am!" Arthur yelled back. "So at least there is one thing we can agree on!"

"Stop that petty quarreling," said a voice from the back of the dungeon.

It was a gentle voice but worn out, probably from unhappiness and age.

"It is useless to mistreat this poor boy or these faithful prison bars. No one has ever escaped from a prison in Necropolis," added the stranger from the darkness.

Arthur searched the shadows for the owner of the tired voice. He could see a silhouette: a man lying down on his side at the very back of the cell, with only the curve of his back visible. *Probably a poor madman*, thought Arthur, because you would have to be in order to stay in this place and not try any escape. He headed back toward the bars.

"Don't tire yourself out. Save your strength if you want to eat," the old man interjected again.

Arthur was forced to admit that he was not making much progress with the bars. He approached the old man instead, intrigued by his advice.

"What do you mean? Eating is not that complicated. Why is it necessary to conserve energy for it?" asked Arthur.

"If you want to eat," explained the old man, still keeping his back turned, "you have to teach them something new. If you don't, you don't eat. And it's impossible to cheat! I have tried to give them old inventions, even a full year later, but it doesn't work. Those morons really have good memories. It is probably their only good quality.

"But that is the rule. They will fill your belly on the one hand, and empty your brain on the other. Knowledge is the only thing of value here, and sleep, the only luxury," he added before trying to find a more comfortable position in which to continue his nap.

Arthur scratched his head, intrigued. There was something about the old man's voice which, while not entirely familiar, reminded him of something or someone. . . .

"What kind of things do they want to know?" asked Arthur, hoping for both an answer and a chance to listen again to that voice.

"Psht! They aren't very observant—they will take anything!" said the old man. "From the laws of physics and mathematics to how to cook green peas. From theorems to mint tea," he added with humor.

This glimmer of a joke surprised Arthur. He had known only one person capable of keeping this kind of perspective in a similar situation . . . a person who was very dear to him and who had disappeared a long time ago.

"I have taught them how to read, to write, to draw—"

"To paint?" added Arthur, who hardly dared to believe it. Could this old man be his grandfather Archibald, who had disappeared four years ago? How would he recognize him, if not by his voice?

Arthur had been only six when his grandfather had disappeared, and the picture in his memory was somewhat fuzzy with age. Now that Archibald was half an inch tall and resembled a Minimoy, it would be almost impossible to recognize him.

The old man was clearly intrigued by Arthur's last words.

"What did you say, my boy?" he asked politely.

"You taught them how to draw and to paint giant canvasses

to fool the enemy, didn't you? Also how to transport water, to direct light using large mirrors—"

"How can this snip of a boy know so much?" the old man wondered aloud. He turned around to see his questioner's face.

Arthur looked at the old face, with its overgrown beard, two funny dimples, an eye that still twinkled, and small wrinkles in the corners of his mouth from smiling too much. There was no doubt—this somewhat crumpled Minimoy was none other than Archibald, his grandfather!

"Because I am the grandson of this great inventor," replied Arthur, beginning to feel a rush of emotion.

"Arthur?" the old man asked tentatively, as if he were asking for the moon.

His grandson smiled a big smile and nodded.

Archibald could not believe his eyes. Life had just sent him the most beautiful of all presents. He rose and threw himself into Arthur's arms.

"Oh! My grandson! My Arthur! I am so happy to see you again," he cried between outbursts of emotion. They hugged each other so tightly that they could hardly breathe. "I have prayed so long to see you again, just once! What joy to finally see my prayers answered!"

A tear rolled down his cheek, disappearing into the wrinkles on his aged face. Then he held Arthur at arm's length to have a better look at him. He stared at him with enormous pride and happiness.

"How you have grown, Arthur! It's incredible!"

"I feel more like I have gotten smaller!" Arthur answered.

"Yes, that's true!" Archibald agreed, and the two began to laugh.

The old man had to hug his grandson again, since he still could not believe what was happening. He wanted to be sure it wasn't Maltazard's idea of a bad joke, one of his famous magic tricks—that this wasn't all an illusion.

But Arthur's arms were really flesh and bone, and now well-muscled. He was no longer the child Archibald remembered. Now he was a handsome young boy, made mature for his age by this adventure. Archibald was really impressed by his grandson.

"But how did you get here?" he asked finally.

"Well, I found your riddle!" Arthur replied.

"Oh, yes, of course! I had completely forgotten I left it for you."

"And the Bogo-Matassalai came to help me with the passage," Arthur added.

"They came all the way from Africa, just to save me?" Archibald wondered.

"Why, yes. I think they like you very much. They entrusted me with the mission of freeing you."

"They did the right thing." Archibald was delighted. "This is wonderful! You're a real hero! I am so proud of you!" He pulled his grandson toward his cot and made him sit down, as if they were in his own living room. "All right, tell me everything! What is new? I want to know everything about you!"

Arthur didn't really know where to start when everything was so complicated. He decided to begin at the end.

"Well, I'm married."

"Really?" Archibald replied with astonishment. This was not at all the news he was expecting. "How old are you?"

"Almost one thousand years old!" Arthur replied.

"Ah, yes! It's true," said Archibald, smiling.

This reminded him of the young Arthur who, at the age of four, had wanted a Swiss army knife, believing that he was old enough to cut his own meat all by himself. His grandfather had replied that at four years, he was already very big, but to have your own knife, you had to be very old.

"And what age do you have to be, to be old!" little Arthur had asked him, who even then would not allow himself to be tricked.

"Ten years!" Archibald had replied, to give himself some time.

Time had now caught up with them.

"And who is the lucky girl?" Grandpa asked.

"Princess Selenia," Arthur said, hardly daring to reveal his pride.

"I couldn't ask for a more adorable granddaughter-in-law!" Archibald rejoiced. "Have you met her family?"

Arthur pointed to Beta, who was sleeping by the bars.

"Ah, brave Betameche!" said Archibald. "I didn't recognize him. I have to say that this is the first time I have seen him so quiet. You must be a good influence on him."

Arthur shrugged.

"My little Arthur, married to a princess!" Archibald couldn't get over it. "That means you are the future king, my son! King Arthur," he said solemnly.

Arthur was embarrassed. He was not used to receiving so many compliments.

"A king in prison is not much of a king," he said. "Come on, Grandpa! We've got to get out of here!"

Arthur jumped up. With his energy and his grandfather's genius, how could they not manage to escape from this blasted prison? But Archibald didn't move.

"And your grandmother? How is your grandmother?" he asked, ignoring Arthur's request.

"She misses you a lot. Now come on!" Arthur answered.

"Of course, of course . . . and the house? How is the house? And the garden? Has she taken care of it?"

"The garden is perfect! But if we are not back by tomorrow noon with the treasure, none of it will be ours anymore—not the garden, not the house!" Arthur insisted, pulling him by the sleeve.

"Of course, my son, of course . . . and the garage? You haven't made a mess, have you? You loved to tinker when you were little!" Archibald remembered. Arthur stood in front of him, grabbed him by the shoulders, and shook him like a sleepwalker.

"Grandpa? Didn't you hear what I said?"

Archibald sighed. "Of course I heard you, Arthur, but . . . no one escapes from the prisons of Necropolis. It has never happened," he said sadly.

"We'll see about that! In the meantime, do you know where the treasure is?"

Archibald nodded. "The treasure is in the throne room and M. the cursed sits on top of it."

"Not for long," promised Arthur, whose spirit had returned. "Selenia went to take care of him and, knowing her, there won't be much left of that terrible Maltazard when she's through!"

Betameche awoke with a start upon hearing the evil name, with all its bad luck. Why was it always when he was asleep that Arthur put his foot in his mouth?

Archibald said a silent prayer, hoping to ward off the bad luck, but it was already too late. Misfortune never waits. The door of the prison opened, and Selenia was thrown in, landing flat on the ground.

One of the henchmen quickly locked the door, and the patrol moved off.

Arthur hurried over to Selenia and hugged her. He wiped her face, which was covered with dust, and fixed her hair.

Selenia was touched by this attention, and she allowed him to continue.

"I failed, Arthur. I'm sorry," she said with infinite sadness.

Never had the princess felt such despair. "All is lost," she added, letting her tears fall where they wanted.

Arthur wiped them away gently with the tips of his fingers.

"As long as we are alive and we have each other . . . nothing is lost," he said.

Selenia smiled at him, impressed by his relentless optimism. She had obviously made the right choice in selecting a husband. Arthur had goodness, generosity, courage, and tenacity—all those qualities that make someone a real prince. Selenia looked deep into his eyes.

The problem was that when Selenia looks at you like that, nothing else in the world matters. Arthur looked at her and melted like a lump of ice tossed into a fire. He leaned forward without even realizing it. Their mouths came closer while their eyelids closed gently.

Just as their lips were about to find each other, Betameche slipped a hand between them.

"Sorry to bother you but . . . I think it would be a good idea, despite the situation, to respect protocol and tradition," he said, annoyed at having to be the grown-up here.

These few words awakened our young princess, who instantly emerged from the dream into which she was slipping. She cleared her throat, stood up, and arranged her torn clothing.

"He is a thousand percent correct! What was I thinking?"

The real princess, the official one, was back. Arthur was

frustrated, like a kitten that has lost its ball.

"But . . . what tradition?" he asked, lost.

"It's an ancestral tradition, a basic rule of protocol that all marriages must follow," the princess explained.

"Yes?" said Arthur.

"Once the first kiss has been given, the one that seals the destiny of the young couple forever, you have to wait a thousand years before the second kiss," recited the princess, who knew protocol better than anyone. Knowing these sorts of things was part of the requirements of being a princess.

"The second kiss will thereby be even stronger, because that which is rare is valuable," she added, completing the picture for Arthur, who was feeling a little overwhelmed by this news.

"Uh . . . yes . . . of course," he muttered.

The door to the prison opened suddenly, so violently that everyone jumped. Darkos was very fond of this kind of theatrical entrance. He loved to play villains who came onstage always at the worst moment, throwing a monkey wrench into the plot.

"How are you all? Not too hot?" he said, detaching a piece of ice that was hanging from the ceiling and putting it into his mouth.

"The temperature is perfect," replied Selenia who, in spite of the cold, was seething inside.

"My father has prepared a little celebration for you. You four are the guests of honor," announced Darkos.

As usual, several henchmen cackled. The guests knew perfectly well what kind of spectacle was awaiting them.

Arthur leaned toward Selenia. "We must provoke a fight. During the confusion, some of us might be able to escape," he whispered into Selenia's ear.

"Comments, young man?" interrupted Darkos, who was following his father's instructions to remain vigilant.

"It's nothing! Arthur just made a relevant observation," Selenia replied.

It was as if she had thrown a worm in front of a fish and asked him not to eat it. Darkos took the bait without hesitation.

"And what was the subject of this relevant observation?" he asked.

"*You* are the subject, obviously," the princess replied.

Darkos beamed. Without his even realizing it, his chest expanded with pride.

"Now that I know the subject, may I have the verb?" he said with poetic spirit.

"Interest. There's the verb that goes with your subject. Arthur was wondering how your father, who is already so ugly, managed to have a son who is even more repugnant than himself. Arthur formulated his sentence in the following manner: 'Darkos's ugliness interests me!' Subject, verb, complement," the princess explained, as if she were an eminent grammarian.

Darkos froze, fixed to his spot. His ice cube fell out of his mouth.

His troop of henchmen began to guffaw, as they often did. Darkos did an about-face and glared at his men. His look was more cutting than a razor blade and the laughter died down quickly.

As best he could, Darkos contained the anger within him, even though it was waiting to explode like a bottle of soda about to be uncapped.

The cursed son took a deep breath.

He turned toward Selenia and smiled, very proud of not having reacted to this insult.

"The pain that awaits you will be nothing compared with the pleasure that awaits me when I see you destroyed," Darkos promised her. "Now, if Her Highness would please take the trouble to follow me."

No fight in sight . . .

"Good try," whispered Arthur to Selenia, who looked disappointed at having failed again.

The little troop lined up and all left the prison together.

"This impromptu ceremony doesn't sound good!" commented Archibald, who was disturbed and impressed by the number of guards.

"At least we're out of the prison—that's not too bad!" Arthur replied, always positive. "We must keep watch for any mistake on their part. That is our only chance."

"This is not exactly the kind of house to make mistakes!" interjected Beta, as worried as Archibald.

"Everyone makes mistakes. Even Achilles had heels!" replied Arthur confidently.

Arthur, Archibald, and now Achilles. Betameche wondered about this new member of the family that he had not yet had the honor of meeting.

"Is he your cousin?" asked Beta.

Archibald felt he should explain. "Achilles was a brave hero of antiquity," he said, "known for his strength and courage. He was almost invulnerable. Only one part of his body was weaker than the others and could be harmed: his heel. So you see, every man has his weakness, even Achilles . . . even Maltazard," Grandpa whispered in Beta's ear. Beta shivered at the sound of the name. He hoped they were right.

CHAPTER
10

At least ten henchmen were needed to push open each of the two doors that led into the large royal hall. The little troop of visitors stayed together as a group and watched with interest as the two enormous metal plates grated mechanically and revealed the entryway.

The hall was gigantic, impressive. It resembled a cathedral. Two huge tanks were attached to the ceiling, like twin clouds caught between mountains. These were, in fact, the double tanks containing subterranean reservoir water that supplied the house. From this perspective, they seemed monstrous. The reservoirs were pierced with dozens of holes, each holding one of Arthur's stolen straws. The multicolored tubes were connected to each other and joined at the center like an enormous pipe system.

Maltazard's plan was now all too clear: he was going to use the straws to guide this vast amount of water into the system of pipes leading to the Minimoy village. He was going to drown them all. The flood would quickly wipe them out since, as everyone remembers, Minimoys do not know how to swim.

"To think I was the one who taught them how to transport water. And now they will use it against my friends," Archibald said sadly as they were marched past his work.

"To think I was the one who provided the straws!" added Arthur, who felt just as responsible.

The little group crossed the monumental, endless pathway.

On each side stood an impressive army of henchmen, standing attentively at their posts. At the end of the esplanade was a pyramid, almost transparent and tinted red. Up close, it proved to be hundreds of pieces of translucent stone, piled upon each other.

At the bottom of this glass monument was a throne, which was much too pretentious looking to belong to a good king.

Maltazard had placed his hands on the armrests, which ended in enormous sculpted skulls. He held himself straight at the back of his throne, not out of pride, but simply because it was the only position that his sick, mutilated body would allow him to assume.

"You were searching for the treasure. There it is!" Archibald whispered into his grandson's ear.

Arthur did not understand. He looked all around them, then at the strange pyramid. He realized he was looking at a pile of precious stones: a hundred rubies, each more perfect that the other, placed scientifically in order to form a perfect pyramid.

Arthur's mouth dropped open. He couldn't believe his eyes. "I *found* it!" he cried jubilantly.

"Finding it is one thing. Transporting it is another story," said Betameche with unusual common sense.

In fact, the treasure was resting on a large platter-shaped disk, and each stone probably weighed several tons to someone Minimoy sized. Arthur thought about it. If only he were his normal size, carrying this saucer full of rubies would be child's play. What he really needed was a way to remember the location of the treasure in the real world, so he would be able to find it again once he had returned to his normal size.

Unfortunately, everything was disproportionate in the world of the Minimoys, and the signs were unrecognizable. Nothing that he saw around here reminded him of anything.

Darkos brought him out of his reverie by pushing him violently in the back. "Advance. Don't keep the master waiting!" Darkos barked, like a good watchdog.

"How sweet, my good and faithful Darkos," interjected Maltazard, like an understanding master. "Forgive him, he is a little nervous right now. His mission was to exterminate your people and, unfortunately, he failed to do so on many occasions. This has made him a bit . . . very bad. But everything will be back in order soon. Papa is here." Maltazard was all too aware of his superior situation and he was savoring it, the way one takes one's time when eating chocolate icing from a cupcake.

"Now . . . let the festivities begin," he exclaimed. He snapped his fingers, and the music began. It was booming, royal music.

Archibald put his fingers in his ears. "If I ever return to prison, I promise to teach them music theory," said the old man, yelling in order to be heard.

Maltazard gestured with his arm. To the side of the ruby pyramid stood a console and a control panel with a dozen large wooden levers. In front of the console, ready to activate the levers, stood a sad little mole.

"Mino?" exclaimed Beta, recognizing his young friend. It was Miro's son Mino, who everyone believed to be lost. He was alive!

This news greatly cheered up Selenia and her brother, who, when they were little, used to spend whole days playing with the little mole. Their favorite game was hide-and-seek, even though Mino would always win because of his ability to dig tunnels. The three had often spent nights stretched out on sele-nielle petals, organizing the stars in order to give them names. They had been inseparable until the day that Mino fell into a trap laid for him by Darkos.

Betameche tried to signal to him now, but the little mole, like all members of his family, did not have very good eyesight. All he could see was a vague form gesturing in the distance. Luckily, his sense of smell was much better than his sight, and soon Selenia's perfume reached his nostrils.

His face lit up and a smile appeared. His friends were there! They had come to his rescue at last. His heart pounded with the promise of freedom.

"Mino, are you awake? I've been signaling you for the last hour," cried Maltazard, as impatient as a hungry shark.

Mino panicked. "Oh, yes! Of course, master! Right away, master," he replied, bending over the controls.

Darkos leaned toward his father. "He can't see very well. They are all like that in his family," he explained. His father gave him an angry look. You do not explain things to Maltazard. Darkos had forgotten. He took a step back, and bowed his head in apology.

"There is nothing that Maltazard does not know. I *am* knowledge, and, unlike yours, my flawless memory has no limits!" his father said to him sternly.

"Excuse me, Father, for that moment of forgetfulness," his son responded, overcome with shame.

"Send," Maltazard bellowed at Mino.

The little mole jumped, hesitating over which lever to use. Finally, he pulled on one that sent a mechanism into operation—a complicated system involving gears, cords, and pulleys.

"I am so happy to see him alive!" whispered Betameche, his face full of joy.

"When you work for Maltazard, you are not really alive—

only on probation!" replied Archibald, who knew what he was talking about.

Slowly a small trapdoor swung open at the top of the gallery, revealing a glimpse of the outside world above ground. A ray of sunlight shone through, forming a well of light. It illuminated the very top of the pyramid, where the largest ruby of all was placed, and began to spread, reflecting off each of the gems' facets. It was as if magic were lighting the pyramid, little by little, from top to bottom, turning it a luminous red . . . like translucent blood traveling through crystal veins.

The show was magnificent, and our friends, despite their precarious situation, couldn't help but appreciate it.

The ray finished its course by lighting the last ruby, the one in which Maltazard's throne was carved.

His whole body was lit up like a divine apparition.

A murmur rose from the assembled army. Some of the soldiers even fell to their knees. This was the kind of magic trick that always impressed weak minds, and Maltazard, as a good dictator, knew them all.

Only Archibald, the old scientist, was unimpressed.

"Well, Archibald! Are you proud of how we have used your knowledge?" Maltazard inquired.

"It's very pretty! It doesn't do much except give you a little color in your cheeks, but it's very pretty," Grandpa answered.

The prince of darkness stiffened, but decided not to get angry.

"Perhaps you prefer my new irrigation system?" he said ironically.

"It is actually very clever and well executed," Archibald confessed. "It's a pity that you plan to use it so wrongly!"

"What? Isn't it designed to transport water?" asked Maltazard, pretending to be naïve.

"Transport water, yes, to irrigate plants and cool people off, but not to flood them!" said the scientist.

"Not only to flood them, my dear Archibald. Also to drown them, pulverize them, liquefy them, do them in, and *annihilate them forever*," said Maltazard with great excitement.

"You are a monster, Maltazard," the old man told him calmly.

"Your granddaughter-in-law said the same thing! Who do you think you are? What gives you the right to divert nature from the path that it is given, but no one else? How dare you claim that nature can be improved by your inventions?"

Archibald was struck speechless. Maltazard had made a point.

"That's the problem with you scientists—you invent things without even taking the time to think through the consequences!" Maltazard went on. "Nature takes years to make a decision. It causes a flower to grow and tests it for millions of years before knowing if it has its place in the grand scheme of things. You invent things and you call yourselves 'geniuses' and you engrave your names in the stones of the pantheon of science!" Maltazard emitted a scornful laugh.

Darkos did also, to imitate his father, even if he had under-stood nothing of what was said.

"It is pure arrogance!" added the dictator with disdain.

"Arrogance is dangerous, but not fatal, my dear Maltazard. Fortunately for you, because otherwise you would already have died a thousand times per day," Archibald shot back.

The sovereign didn't react, but these insults were beginning to get to him.

"I'll take that as a compliment, since arrogance is a require-ment for every great ruler!" Maltazard said.

"Being a ruler is not only about a title. You must know how to behave like one, to know how to be good, just, and gener-ous," Archibald said firmly.

"What a portrait! It sounds exactly like me," joked Maltazard. Darkos laughed. For once he had understood the joke. "Well, I am going to prove to you that I *can* be good and generous. You are free to go," he announced, accompanying his words with a sweeping theatrical gesture.

Several henchmen had raised the grille that blocked the main pipe system. These pipes led directly to the Minimoy vil-lage, and it was here that all the straws were aimed. Archibald understood the trap before any of the others.

"You offer us freedom—and the death that goes along with it!" Archibald said.

"Yes, two gifts at a time. Aren't I ever so generous?" answered Maltazard.

"The minute we step through that gate, you will release tons of water on us!" exclaimed the princess, who had just realized his evil plan.

"You should think less, Selenia, and run more!" he answered cruelly.

"What's the use of running if there is only one chance in a million of surviving?" the princess added.

"One chance in a million? I find that somewhat optimistic. I would say, perhaps, one chance in one hundred million," the dictator specified with humor. "But it's better than nothing, isn't it? Go on! Bon voyage!" Maltazard lifted his arms again and signaled to the henchmen to push the Minimoys into the pipe.

As Betameche began to tremble like a leaf, Arthur finally found the idea he was looking for.

"May I ask your Serene Greatness for one last favor before dying? A very small favor that will only serve to highlight your majesty's extreme graciousness?" he said, bowing low.

"I like that little one!" Maltazard said. He was always easily swayed by flattery. "What is this favor?"

"I would like to leave my only treasure, this bracelet, to my friend Mino, who is over there."

The little mole was completely surprised by the interest that everyone suddenly had in him, especially this young man, who he did not know at all.

Maltazard looked at the watch that Arthur was holding up.

He sniffed, but could not smell a trap of any sort. Finally he announced: "Granted."

The henchmen began to applaud the generosity of their master.

While Maltazard waved happily at his admirers, Arthur walked over to Mino.

"Your father sent me," he whispered into the mole's ear.

He took off his watch and handed it to Mino. "Once I am outside, I need you to send me a signal, so that I will be able to find the treasure. You must send the signal precisely at noon. Is that clear?" Arthur asked urgently.

Mino was astounded. "But how do you want me to do it?"

"With your mirrors, Mino!" Arthur insisted. This was his last hope. "Do you understand?"

Mino, completely lost, agreed with a nod, but it was more to please Arthur than anything else.

"That's enough now. My mercy has its limits! Take them away!" exclaimed Maltazard.

The henchmen grabbed Arthur and hustled him back to his group, now standing at the entrance of the enormous pipe.

Mino watched his new friend move away, bewildered.

"At noon!" whispered Arthur.

The guards pushed the small group inside the pipe. The grille immediately came down behind them, separating them from the square. There was only one exit now.

In front of them was the long pipe that led to freedom . . .

freedom they would never reach. This pipe would also be their tomb.

The idea of inevitable death completely depressed the entire group. No one wanted to run. What for? To delay their suffering by a few seconds? Better to have it over with quickly, so the little group stayed there, worn out, behind the grille.

The spectacle was not a very interesting one and Maltazard sighed.

"All right. I will give you a one-minute head start. That will add a little spice," he said, trying to liven up the game.

Darkos was very excited by this news.

"Bring the timetables," cried Darkos.

Two henchmen brought in an enormous panel. In the center was a nail on which a package of dried leaves had been attached. On the first leaf was the word "sixty."

Selenia, clinging to the bars, glared at Maltazard. There was so much venom in her eyes that she hoped a drop of it could reach him.

"You will pay for this," she murmured between her clenched teeth.

"He already is!" Arthur replied, taking her by the arm. "Hurry, now!"

"What's the use of running?" the princess said, and pulled her arm away. "So we can die a little bit later? I prefer to stand here and die with dignity, staring death in the face!"

Arthur grabbed her more firmly by the arm. "One minute.

That's better than nothing! That gives us the time to come up with something," he cried with conviction.

This was the first time he had been so decisive, and Selenia was quite impressed. Was her awkward prince growing up? she wondered. She allowed herself to be pulled along behind him.

Maltazard was happy to see his four captives start running.

"Finally a bit of sport! Begin the countdown," he ordered with pleasure.

The henchman removed the first leaf, marked "sixty." Underneath was another, marked with a magnificent "fifty-nine."

The clock was so simple and crude it would make a Swiss turn pale, but Maltazard was greatly amused. He even nodded his head in time with the discarded leaves.

"Prepare the valves," he ordered, between two nods.

Darkos left to take his place, wiggling with delight like a fish, while the henchman timekeeper unveiled a new leaf marked with a "fifty-two."

CHAPTER

11

The Minimoys ran as best they could through the garbage and the layer of filth that time had deposited at the bottom of the tunnel. But Archibald tired quickly and he began to slow down. The old man had spent four years in M.'s prisons without any exercise, and the muscles in his poor legs were weak.

"Sorry, Arthur, I can't do it," said the old man, as he came to a stop, breathing heavily. He sat down on some sort of round object, which was attached to another, much bigger object. Arthur turned back and ran up to him.

"Go on! I'll stay here and wait for the end with a bit of dignity," Grandpa sighed.

"That's not possible! I can't leave you here! Come on, Grandpa, give it one more try," Arthur said.

He tugged him gently by the arm, but the old man pulled away.

"What's the use, Arthur? Look at the facts, my boy. We're lost."

With these words, the rest of the group immediately fell

apart. If a scientist thought that the chances for survival were now zero, why bother struggling?

Beta and Selenia slumped to the ground, overcome by sadness.

Arthur sighed. He didn't know what to do.

Maltazard, on the other hand, was in fine spirits, collecting his dead leaves. The one marked "twenty" pleased him a lot. He was practically singing.

"All of this has made me hungry. Is there something to eat? I like to snack during a show," he said, amusing himself like a king.

A henchman immediately brought a large platter of small grilled roaches, His Highness's favorite dish. There was always a plate of these appalling tidbits in every room of the palace. It would probably have been easier for a servant to follow him around all day, carrying a platter, but Maltazard had always refused to have this done. He liked to see his minions scurry around whenever he demanded his treats. That was part of his pleasure—knowing that they would be rushing to bring him his plate as quickly as possible, on pain of death. More even than these small, grilled insects, the suffering of others was his favorite dish.

He did not know that, behind his back, Darkos had hidden plates all over the palace, so that his father would never have to wait too long.

"Cooked just right!" Maltazard pronounced as he nibbled on a roach, which was crusty exactly the way he liked it. Darkos took this as a compliment.

The timekeeper revealed a new leaf: a magnificent "ten."

"Slow down a little!" Maltazard ordered. "I need time to chew!"

Arthur could not concede defeat. He wanted to die a hero, to fight until the end, until the last moment. It had nothing to do with dignity.

So he walked in circles, trying to come up with an idea. "There must be a solution! There is always a solution," he repeated constantly.

"It's not just an idea that we need now, Arthur—it's a miracle," replied Archibald, who had abandoned all hope.

Arthur let out a big sigh. He was seconds away from giving up like the rest of them. He lifted his eyes upward, as if to call for help, as if to ask for a miracle, no matter how small. Something caught his attention. How was it possible that he could see the sky from where he was? He realized that he was standing below a pipe that rose to the surface. Unfortunately, the opening was too high and the walls too slippery to be climbed.

If only that nice spider could return and drop down her thread. Alas, it was not to be. However, the small blades of grass that he saw all around the opening above reminded him of something. This must be the drain hole in his grandmother's garden.

Arthur searched his memory, but he couldn't pinpoint what it was.

Perhaps he was on the wrong track. He looked down at the object on which his grandfather was sitting.

The object was lying in the light, so it had probably fallen from above. From the garden. That triggered something in Arthur's brain. Garden. Pipe. Object. Fall. He leaped forward and pulled his grandfather up.

Archibald had been sitting on the tire of a car, resting on its side. And it was not just any car. It was the magnificent racing car, the red Ferrari, that Arthur had just gotten for his birthday on Saturday, a day which now seemed like ancient history. He remembered now that the dust from Davido's car had knocked the toy into the opening of a drainpipe on Sunday. In all the excitement of searching for the treasure after Davido left, Arthur had forgotten to rescue his present.

"Grandpa! *You're* the miracle," he shouted with joy.

"Explain yourself, Arthur!" Selenia said, astonished.

"This is a car! It's *my* car. Grandma gave it to me. We are saved!" he crowed enthusiastically.

Archibald knit his brows. "Your grandmother has lost all sense of reality. Aren't you still a little too young to be driving this kind of car?"

"When she gave it to me, it was much smaller, I assure you," Arthur replied with a smile from ear to ear. "Help me!" he cried to his partners.

Selenia and Betameche joined him on the other side of the car, which was standing up on its side like a wall. They began to push with all of their strength. With superhuman effort, the car at last fell back on its four wheels. Their cries of joy echoed down the tunnel.

Maltazard was amazed. How could they be happy, when they had only a few seconds left to live? This puzzle disturbed him and he decided not to take any risks. He was too close to victory.

"Open the valves," he ordered suddenly.

"But . . . the counter is not at zero. There are still three leaves," said Darkos, always a little slow on the uptake.

"I know how to count to three!" Maltazard yelled. "Open the valves!"

Darkos ran to the valves to execute his mission before his father decided to execute him.

The henchman timekeeper was quicker than Darkos and he tore off the last leaves all together. "Zero," he cried, with a big smile.

Arthur put the little key, which had become enormous, in the top of the car.

It was so hard to move that beads of sweat began to appear on his forehead. Selenia climbed up beside him and helped him turn the key around and around.

"Are you sure you know how to drive this kind of car?"

Betameche asked. He was uncomfortable with unfamiliar transportation.

"It's my specialty," Arthur answered quickly to avoid further
discussion.

Betameche only half believed him.

Darkos came up to the henchmen posted along the cistern. "Go ahead," *he*
ordered.

The henchmen swung their mallets and knocked loose the
wedges that were temporarily blocking the holes.

Once the wedges were removed, Darkos took a sledgeham-
mer and, with all his strength, slammed it into the tap, which
gave way immediately.

The water instantly began to pour through the straws, as if
they were large veins, and rushed like a torrent through the
pipe taken by our escapees.

Arthur made another attempt to turn the key. Selenia was
blowing on her hands, which were hurting from the effort
she'd put in.

Suddenly the rumble of rushing water reached their ears.
Selenia jumped.

"That's it! They have opened the valves. Arthur, hurry!" she
cried.

"Get in the front. I'll be right behind you," Arthur ordered
as he continued to lean on the key.

Betameche scrambled in and joined Archibald in the back of the car. They both turned and saw, through the back window, the mass of water that was rushing upon them.

"Hurry, Arthur," his grandpa pleaded, frightened by the sight of the enormous wave.

"If we want to be able to reach the end, I must turn the spring as tight as I can," replied Arthur, grimacing with pain. He drew on his last bit of strength, emitting a Herculean cry to give himself courage. He managed to turn the key one more time, under Selenia's watchful—and admiring—eye.

Arthur held the key in place with his shoulder and tried to grab a bit of wood on the ground. He needed something to block the key so he would have time to get into the car, but the wave would wait for no one and it was dangerously close now.

Beta sat with his mouth open and his hands pressed over his eyes. He would have liked to scream for help, but no sound would come out—his jaws were so strained with fear.

Arthur finally managed to plant a stick to temporarily block the key. He jumped into the car, behind the steering wheel.

The interior was rather basic, but Arthur quickly found his bearings. The Ferrari could not be much more complicated than his grandma's Chevrolet. He hoped this car wouldn't end up wrapped around a tree. He adjusted his rearview mirror and saw the liquid wall pounding toward them, ready to swallow them up.

"And we're off," he sang, pulling loose the stick that was blocking the key.

The rear wheels immediately began to spin in place, finally free. Fortunately, the wind generated by the movement of the wave pushed the car forward.

Then the tires finally began to find some traction and the Ferrari doubled its speed. The car flew through the tunnel, fleeing the torrent.

Arthur clutched the steering wheel with both hands. Selenia's back was glued to her seat. Betameche muttered that he would never again take public transportation of any kind; while Archibald, intoxicated by the speed, watched the scenery pass by with delight.

"It's amazing what progress cars have made in only four years," he mused.

The speed had become so fast that the straight line of the pipe now seemed to be a series of successive turns. Arthur concentrated harder. It was no longer a matter of only holding the steering wheel but of actually driving.

Betameche, despite the pressure of the speed, managed to grab on to the back of the front seats, and he pulled himself forward to address Arthur. "At the next intersection, make a right," he said.

He had no sooner finished his sentence than the fork appeared in front of Arthur. He turned the steering wheel sharply to the right, which threw the passengers against the doors.

The car straightened itself up in this new pipe. Arthur breathed a sigh of relief.

"Beta? Try and let me know a little sooner the next time," he said.

"Okay. Left!" cried Betameche.

But the new fork was already there. Arthur yelled with surprise and reflexively spun the steering wheel to the left. They just barely avoided crashing into the beveled wall that separated the two paths.

Arthur let out an even bigger sigh of relief. "Thanks, Beta," he said. He was so tense that sweat from his forehead was dripping into his eyes. Selenia noticed and leaned over to wipe his face with her sleeve. The two lovebirds exchanged smiles.

"Right!" hollered Betameche, making them jump.

Arthur, entranced by Selenia's smile, could barely distinguish his right from his left, and he spun the steering wheel in all directions. It was mere luck that Arthur managed to steer the car into the tunnel on the right.

Their screams echoed throughout the entire network of pipes.

CHAPTER
12

The sun had risen on a sad-looking garden, and it shone in the sky as the minutes ticked along toward noon. Arthur's father, for the thousandth time, put his foot on the shovel and pushed. This was his sixty-seventh consecutive hole.

His wife watched from a distance, hoping to avoid any new catastrophes. All at once she thought she heard something—a small cry that came from somewhere far away and resounded in the air. But it quickly vanished. Arthur's mother continued to listen for a moment, then decided that it was probably her imagination playing tricks on her. She went back to peeling oranges for her husband.

But now another noise could be heard in the air. It was a dull, seething rumble. Arthur's mother listened again. This one was only getting louder.

"Honey, do you hear that strange noise?"

Arthur's father, half asleep on his shovel, stood up. "What, where?" he asked with the expression of a bear emerging from hibernation.

"There, in the ground. It sounds like water spreading underground." She got down on her knees and bent over to better pinpoint the sound that was gurgling deep down inside the earth.

Arthur's father laughed. "Now you're hearing things?" he joked, his elbow on the handle of his shovel. "Just wait a bit and maybe you'll see little angels and spirits everywhere."

He had no idea how right he was. Strange silhouettes suddenly appeared, outlined behind her laughing husband. Arthur's mother saw them and her smile froze.

"Spirits and little monsters, like in your father's old books," Arthur's father added with a chuckle. "With short fur and ugly faces, along with their brothers, the sorcerers."

He began to laugh stupidly, and then to mimic a tribal dance. His wife looked at him, her face contorted with fear. She tried to point toward the shapes behind her husband and ended up fainting into the oranges.

Arthur's father was quite surprised. He turned around to look where she had been pointing and found himself nose to nose, or rather nose to belly button, with five Bogo-Matassalai. They were all dressed in simple loincloths, and each carried a pointed spear in his hand.

Arthur's father instantly turned to jelly. His teeth began to chatter like a typewriter that was printing his last will.

The Bogo-Matassalai chief carefully leaned down to him, which took some time since there was an almost three-foot difference between the two men.

"Do you have the time?" the giant African man asked politely.

Arthur's father nodded rapidly, like a marionette at the end of a string. He looked at his wrist. He was afraid he wouldn't be able to read the watch hands; and, as it happens, he couldn't, since he was not, after all, wearing a watch.

"It is . . . it is . . ."

He tapped on his wrist pointlessly. There was no way he was going to be able to give them the time.

"I—I have another in the kitchen that works better," he stammered, staring at the point of the nearest spear.

The Bogo-Matassalai said nothing and simply smiled.

Arthur's father concluded that he had permission to leave. "I'll—I'll be back," he stuttered, before taking off like a rabbit in the direction of the house.

Darkos proudly read from a small piece of paper in his hand. "According to my calculations, the water should reach the Minimoy village in less than thirty seconds," he announced to his father, who was immensely pleased by the news.

"Perfect, perfect! In less than one minute, I will be the

absolute and uncontested master of the Seven Lands, and the Minimoy people will be nothing more than a mere paragraph in the history books."

Maltazard rubbed his hands evilly.

The king Sifrat de Matradoy paced up and down at the main door to his vil- lage, where our brave adventurers had set out not so long ago. Reports had come in that the Maltazard situation was serious and that the chances of saving his kingdom were infinitesimal. But the loss of a kingdom was nothing compared with the loss of his children. Selenia and Betameche had still not returned and that was the cause of his great concern.

"What time is it, my brave Miro?" he asked the faithful mole.

Miro took his watch out of his pocket, looking unhappy, and squinted at it. "Ten minutes until noon, my king," he replied.

And here there was no question of stretching time, as Maltazard had with his leaf chronometer. In the land of the Minimoys, seconds were regular and led inevitably to an end that in this case would most likely be tragic.

The king sighed. "Only ten minutes left and we still have no news," he noted sadly.

Miro approached and placed his hand affectionately on the king's shoulder. "Have faith, my good king. Your daughter has exceptional courage. And as for young Arthur, he seems resourceful and full of common sense. I am convinced that they will think of something."

The king smiled slightly, comforted by these kind words. "May the gods hear you, my good Miro. May the gods hear you."

Despite his fatigue, Arthur still clutched the steering wheel. He had become used to the speed, and his eyes were glued to the road ahead.

The Ferrari had succeeded in outrunning the wave that was following them—so far.

"Thanks, Grandma," he said softly. Arthur knew he would never have managed without this magnificent gift. His grandmother could not have imagined that a toy would one day be so useful or that it would save the lives of the people most dear to her.

Betameche suddenly turned around. He seemed to have recognized the place in spite of their speed. "I think we are almost there," he said. "That was the border that marks the entrance to the dandelion field."

Selenia peered down the tunnel ahead of them. "There, the door! That's the door to the village!" she screamed with joy.

This news was welcomed with great emotion in the car, and everyone congratulated one another and jumped about. But their happiness was short-lived. The car had begun to slow down.

"Oh, no!" whispered Arthur. The Ferrari slowed down more and finally rolled to a complete stop. There was consternation onboard.

"Do you want me to get out and fix it?" Selenia asked.

Arthur did not think it could be fixed, but he barely had time to say that before Beta cut him off in mid-sentence.

"Hurry! We have to wind the spring before the water reaches us."

"Impossible! It will take too much time. Besides, my arms are still aching all over—I don't think I *could* move it again," Arthur replied.

"Then I hope your legs are in better shape than that," Selenia said, throwing open her door.

In a few seconds, the group had left the car and begun to run down the tunnel toward the Minimoy village. It was no more than half a mile, but it seemed like the ends of the earth. The Ferrari would have covered the distance in a few seconds . . . and so would the wave, whose rumbling could be heard once again.

"Quick! The water is catching up to us," Arthur yelled to his grandfather and Betameche who, overcome with fatigue, were lagging behind.

Inside the city, the sound of the water was beginning to be heard.

"What is that rumbling?" the king asked Miro.

"I have no idea," the mole replied, "but I can feel waves in my feet. This vibration can mean no good."

The little group had only twenty yards left to run. Arthur turned and slipped his arm under his grandfather's. "One last push, okay, Grandpa? I know you can do it," the young man urged.

Arthur had developed a phenomenal and unexpected energy. He, who at home had always had a tendency to avoid household chores using never-to-be-finished homework as an excuse, had now become a completely unrecognizable young man, one who was brave as any warrior.

As they got closer, they could all see that the huge gates to the village were open—waiting for their return—but that there was another layer of secondary safety doors in front of it that was closed and barred. It was the worst possible situation: with the great doors open, the water would destroy the village for certain. But with the smaller doors closed, the four of them would not be able to get in to warn the Minimoys . . . or to escape the flood.

Selenia was the first to arrive at the door, and she began to pound with all her might. "Open the door!" she cried with all the strength she could muster.

A few yards away, the king perked up his ears. He could pick her sweet little voice out of a thousand. It was his beloved daughter, his princess, his heroine who had returned from her mission! He ran back toward the main gate.

The guard slid open the little window into the tunnel. Even though the wave was not yet visible, its wind was already there, and the watchman caught a gust of air right in his face.

"Who goes there?" he asked in a deep voice, hoping it showed he was unafraid.

Selenia put her hand into the opening, then stood on tip-toes to show her face. Betameche ran up and pushed his sister aside to show his.

The watchman looked at them for a moment, expression-less, then slammed the window in their faces.

This made Selenia furious, of course, and she knocked even louder. Arthur and his grandfather joined them, and they all began to pound on the door.

The king arrived at the entrance to the village and was sur-prised that the watchman was not reacting to this din. "What are you doing? Why haven't you opened this door?"

"It's another trick," explained the watchman. "But they won't do that to me a second time! This time, they made a drawing—an animated one—of Princess Selenia and Prince Betameche. The one of the princess is particularly well done, but the one of Betameche has a few mistakes and you can tell right away that it's a fake."

The little group outside continued to pound with all their

strength, while the wind preceding the torrent became stronger and stronger.

Archibald turned to estimate how much time they had left. He was amazed to see that the wave was already visible. A wall of furious water was headed in their direction at rocket speed.

"Open the door, for goodness sake!" Archibald cried out suddenly, his survival instinct finally awoken.

The king heard this urgent cry. If his memory served him correctly, it was the voice of Archibald! The king approached the door. He wanted to be sure.

He opened the little window and instantly saw the faces of Selenia and Betameche. "Help!" they cried in unison, their faces distorted with fear.

The king, furious, turned quickly toward the watchman.

"Open this door immediately, you triple gamoul," he cried with all his powerful authority. The watchman ran toward the door and, with the help of his comrades, unlocked the sliding latches.

"Hurry up!" urged Betameche, who was watching the monstrous wave swallow the Ferrari in less than a second. The wind was now so strong that it plastered our heroes against the door.

The last lock was finally removed and the guardians began to open the door, but the wind surprised everyone by bursting the doors open all of a sudden. Our friends ran inside and quickly placed themselves behind the enormous main doors.

"Quick! The wave is coming! Help us close the gate," cried Arthur without taking the time to greet anyone.

The watchman was somewhat annoyed. "Open, close—they don't know what they want!" he muttered.

Just then he saw the wave, seething with foam, hurtling toward them. His attitude changed immediately, and he ran to Arthur's side. "Come on! Help!" he cried to his fellow guards, who immediately came to his aid.

There were ten of them to push the doors, ten who were sorry that it was so heavy and that the wind was so violent. As for the wave, it seemed delighted to have finally found its destination and thrilled at the idea of drowning everything.

Miro threw himself against the door with the guards. The little mole was more accustomed to digging tunnels than to pushing doors, but, in the event of an extreme emergency like the present one, any assistance was welcome.

"Come on, my good Palmito, put me down!" the king instructed his animal carrier.

With its powerful hands, Palmito took the king carefully by his head and placed him delicately on the ground.

"Come on, Palmito, close this door for me!"

Palmito looked at him for two seconds with his gentle look.

It always took the animal two seconds to understand what was being said. The Minimoy language was not its native tongue. People had a tendency to forget that.

Finally the animal put its enormous hand on the door and pushed with its huge muscled arms. The wave was getting closer. It was only a few yards away.

Arthur jumped on the first latch and pushed it through the rings.

The wave began to crash against the door with an unexpected violence. The shock could be felt everywhere, and our little friends were thrown to the ground.

Arthur struggled up and reached the second latch, which he wrestled to close.

On the other side, the water filled the entire tunnel. Not a bubble of air remained.

The second bar finally slid into the rings and held the door fast. Everyone kept their hands on the door just in case, to give added support. This was necessary, since the pressure from the water on the other side was enormous.

Water is powerful but also clever. It could take advantage of the smallest crevice to infiltrate the interior.

The king saw that the door was completely and firmly closed.

"Let us hope it will resist," he said with some concern.

✳ ✳ ✳

Darkos looked at his abacus. The last round ball rolled gently on the two rods that guided it, indicating the end of the cycle.

"That's it," he said with a great deal of pleasure. He turned toward his father. "From this moment on, Your Majesty, you are the one and only emperor. You rule as absolute master over all of the Seven Lands."

Darkos bowed more deeply than usual. Maltazard savored his success. He slowly expanded his chest, as if he were breathing for the first time, then sighed with pleasure.

"Even though I do not care much for honors, I must acknowledge that it does mean something to know that you are the master of the world," he admitted with due modesty. "But what pleases me most of all . . . is to know that all my enemies are dead!" he added with glee.

Our little heroes weren't exactly dead yet, but the situation remained precarious.

"Do you think the door will hold?" asked the king, who liked to be reassured.

"It will hold for now," Miro replied. "We should get everyone to hold the door later, when the pressure starts building up. But for now, we are safe."

Coming from an engineer as well-known as Miro, this response satisfied everyone.

Selenia and Betameche slowly let go of the door and ran into the waiting arms of their father.

"My children, what joy to know you are safe and sound!" the king exclaimed, overcome with emotion. He hugged them close to his chest and raised his head toward the heavens, his eyes full of tears.

"Thank you! Thank you for having answered my prayers!" he said with deep humility.

CHAPTER
13

Grandma would also have liked to have her prayers answered. She was on her third since morning, with no results yet.

She gave a small sigh at the same moment Arthur's father chose to burst into the living room, babbling like a Martian.

"There! There! They are giants! Too many! Five! In the garden! Warriors! Very tall! And they don't know what time it is!" he shouted as if he were delivering a telegram.

He whirled around, gasping for air.

"Quick! Very angry! No time to lose!" he added before heading toward the door.

He had not come to find out the time, as he had led the Bogo-Matassalai to believe. He had come to find an escape route.

Arthur's father peeked through the window curtain and saw that the visitors were still in the garden. It was the perfect moment to flee.

"I'll . . . be back," he managed to say to Grandma, before

sprinting to the front door on the other side of the house. He opened the door and jumped again. There was another visitor, or rather three visitors, to be exact.

The first one was actually fairly elegant. Arthur's father calmed down a bit as Davido doffed his hat. The other two wore rather frightening-looking uniforms—police uniforms.

"It is noon!" Davido said with a big smile, as if he had just won the lottery.

Arthur's father looked at them without understanding. Davido took out his watch, carefully chained to his vest.

"Five minutes *to* noon, to be precise," he added with humor. "This is the limit of my patience."

Betameche led the group as they bolted into the Hall of Passages.

The old watchman was once again disturbed and had to leave his cocoon. This did not put him in a very good mood.

"Hurry up! I've already turned the first ring," he grumbled. "You have less than four minutes!"

Archibald positioned himself in front of the giant mirror, behind the lens of the magic telescope. The king was there to say good-bye. He had come without Palmito, who was too big for the Hall of Passages.

The king approached Archibald. The two men smiled knowing smiles and shook hands.

"No sooner have you returned than you have to leave us," said the king with a sadness that was difficult for him to hide.

"It's the law of the stars and stars don't wait!" Archibald answered with a regretful smile.

"I know, and it's a real pity. There are so many things that you still have to teach us!" the king said with great humility.

Archibald placed his hand on the king's shoulder. "You have your own wealth of knowledge in addition to what I have taught you," he said. "The two of us, we form a whole, the knowledge of one complementing the knowledge of the other. Isn't that the secret of teamwork? The secret of the Minimoys?" Grandpa said gently.

"Yes, that is true," admitted the king. "'The more we are, the more we laugh.' Fiftieth commandment."

"See, it is you who taught me that," Archibald said with a big smile.

The king was greatly moved by this mark of friendship and respect. The two men, small in size but great in heart, shook hands vigorously.

The gatekeeper turned the second ring, that of the mind.

"Take good care of my son-in-law," the king said with a smile.

"With pleasure. And you, take good care of my grand-daughter-in-law," Archibald replied.

The gatekeeper finished turning the third ring, that of the soul.

"All aboard," he cried, like a conductor.

Archibald waved one last time and threw himself on the glass, which immediately absorbed him. The old man disappeared, like a piece of toast under jelly.

Arthur watched as his grandfather, tossed by magic, passed through each of the lenses, becoming larger each time. The end of the telescope spit him out like a piece of dust that expands when it makes contact with the air and the light.

Within three rolls in the thick grass, Archibald had resumed his normal size.

He took a deep breath and decided to remain for a few moments on the ground, trying to put his emotions in order. The Bogo-Matassalai chief stood over him. The man greeted him with a magnificent smile, showing all his beautiful white teeth.

"Did you have a good trip, Archibald?" asked the chief.

"Magnificent! A little long but . . . magnificent," Grandpa replied, comforted to see his old friend.

"And Arthur?" wondered the African.

"He's coming!"

Our Minimoy friends were not too eager to see their brave Arthur leave, and he also was not keen to disappear into the gelatinous mass of the telescope lenses. But that was the price he had to pay if he was to return to his family and tell his grandma all about his adventures.

Betameche approached him, visibly moved. "It will be so

boring without you! Come back soon," begged the little prince.

"As soon as I can—at the seventh moon next year. It's a promise," Arthur replied, raising his hand as a pledge.

Betameche was somewhat surprised by this custom, but it pleased him and he immediately adopted it.

"Promise," said Betameche, raising his hand in a mirror gesture.

Arthur could not help but laugh.

"We have to hurry," the gatekeeper reminded him. "The passage will close in thirty seconds!"

Arthur stood in front of the enormous lens that distorted his reflection.

Selenia approached, somewhat shyly. She had a hard time containing her emotions. "It took me a thousand years to choose a husband and then I only had him for a few hours," the princess said, trying not to cry.

"I have to go back. You know that. My family must be so worried, just as yours was," Arthur said.

"Of course, of course," Selenia agreed without much conviction.

"And twelve moons isn't so long," Arthur added, trying to be reassuring.

"Twelve moons! That's *millions* of seconds that I will spend without you," said Selenia, who could no longer hold back her tears.

Arthur's eyes were also swimming. With the tip of his finger he collected her tears and kissed them.

"Millions of seconds. It will be a good test of our love," he said. "The people who wrote your rules would approve."

"You know what?" the princess said. "I don't give a hump-backed gamoul about protocol." She leaned forward and her lips met Arthur's in a second kiss, even more real than the first.

Then Selenia placed her hands on Arthur's shoulders and pushed him back.

Arthur disappeared, absorbed by the glass that was waiting for him. "Selenia," he managed to call before his voice was muffled by the glass and he was tossed to and fro by the uncontrollable currents.

Now he understood what mountain climbers feel, caught in monstrous avalanches. Arthur struggled and did not stop moving, as was recommended in *The Guide to Mountain Climbing*, his favorite book before he found his grandfather's accounts of his African adventures.

The lenses that he was passing through became smaller and smaller, harder and harder. The last one was like a wall and Arthur's head hurt passing through it.

As soon as he emerged, his lungs filled with pure air. His entire body inflated like a balloon, like a car's air bag after an accident. He was thrown to the ground, and he rolled away. He ended up on all fours in the grass, face-to-face with a dog's nose.

Alfred, delighted to see his master, licked Arthur's face and wagged his tail vigorously. Arthur burst out laughing and tried to protect himself from these dribbling assaults.

"Stop it, Alfred! Let me breathe for a few seconds," said Arthur, thrilled to see his faithful friend again.

Archibald came to the rescue and offered him a hand.

As soon as Arthur stood up, he saw his mother, still passed out nearby. Arthur ran toward her and bent over her. "What happened?" he asked worriedly.

"She saw us and fainted into the oranges," the Bogo-Matassalai chief explained simply, holding up the fruit as proof.

Arthur gazed at his mother's face with affection. "Wake up, Mom! It's me," he whispered in a voice so irresistibly charming that his mother awoke at once. She slowly opened her eyes and saw the face of her son right in front of her. At first she thought that she must be dreaming, so she smiled blissfully and lowered her eyelids again.

"Mom," Arthur insisted, tapping her on the cheek.

His mother's eyes flew open. "This isn't a dream?" she asked with a look of amazement.

"Of course not! It's me, Arthur! Your son," he said, shaking her lightly by the shoulders.

Arthur's mother realized that her son had really returned, and she immediately burst into tears. "Oh, my dear little boy," she said and promptly fainted into the oranges again.

At the other side of the garden, Grandma was unaware of the drama that was unfolding as she came out onto the front steps, where Davido was standing. The loathsome landlord peered with exaggerated care at the small road winding off toward the horizon. He looked again at his watch, like an official timekeeper.

"Noon on the dot," he gleefully declared to his audience of one. "Noon on the dot and still *no one* on the horizon," he added, to twist the knife in the wound.

He let out a big sigh before adding with false desperation, "I am afraid that even on this beautiful day, there won't be any miracle!"

He took advantage of the fact that his back was to Grandma in order to laugh stupidly. He would have made an excellent henchman for Maltazard.

The two policemen stood by, helpless. They wanted so much to help this poor woman, but today the law was on Davido's side and the policemen, unfortunately, had to do their job.

Davido's villainous smile faded and he became serious. Clearing his throat, he turned toward Grandma and discovered that she was no longer alone. Archibald and Arthur were on either side of her, each holding her by the arm. They had appeared as if by magic.

Davido was speechless. His jaw dropped.

Grandma, on the other hand, looked radiant. Her two most beloved people in all the world had returned to her at last.

If Harry Houdini himself had made an entire village disappear in front of his eyes, Davido could not have been more astonished. This was more than a magic trick. It was more than a miracle. It was a catastrophe.

Archibald smiled. It was not a friendly smile but a polite one. "You are right, Davido. . . . It is a very beautiful day," the old man exclaimed.

Davido, paralyzed by surprise, could not move.

"I believe we have certain papers to sign?" Grandpa asked him.

Davido took a few seconds to respond. The shock had obviously damaged his poor mental capacities, which were already rather limited.

"Let's go into the living room. It's cooler there and we will be more comfortable," Archibald suggested with exaggerated courtesy. As he turned toward the house, he whispered a few words into Arthur's ear, as discreetly as possible.

Here is what he said: "Now is when we need the treasure. I'll create a diversion and try to gain some time. You take care of finding the rubies!"

Arthur was not sure that his was the easier mission, but this mark of confidence made him very proud. "You can count on me," he answered just as discreetly. He headed toward the back of the garden, his head held high.

He had only gone a few yards when he tripped and fell into one of the holes dug by his father, landing face-first.

Alfred poked in his nose to check out the damages.

"It's not over yet," Arthur sputtered through a mouthful of dirt.

CHAPTER
14

In the great square of Necropolis, the time had come to prepare for war.

The army of henchmen was lined up, forming an immense M on the ground.

There were thousands of soldiers perched on their mosquito mounts, preparing to invade new lands.

Maltazard came slowly out onto his balcony, which overlooked the enormous square where his perfect army had assembled. For the occasion, he had put on a new cape, in deep black with hundreds of shining stars, each glittering more brightly than the other.

The noise of the army greeted their powerful ruler, who reached out his arms toward his people.

The Prince of Darkness is savoring his overwhelming, disgusting victory, thought Mino, still standing near the pyramid, as he wondered what to do. Could Arthur have survived such a tidal wave?

It was practically impossible, but it was not the "impossible" that bothered him, it was the "practically." Even if there was only one chance in a million, there was still a chance and Mino did not want to waste it.

Mino looked at the watch again. Although the little mole was perfectly able to tell time, he was, unfortunately, incapable of reading something so close to his face. He panicked. It didn't even work to hold his arm as far away from his body as possible. He was blind as a mole.

Arthur paced up and down the garden in every direction. It was impossible to recognize anything from the land of the Minimoys at the moment, except the tiny stream that he had traveled on aboard his nutshell. He followed it, along the little wall, only a few bricks high, and arrived at the foot of the windmill.

There must be a minuscule grille, somewhere, buried in the grass, but try as he might, Arthur couldn't find it. Alfred, on the other hand, had found his ball, the new one he had just given to Arthur for his birthday. He placed it at the feet of his master, who, as far as the dog could tell, was looking everywhere for it.

"This is not the time to play, Alfred," said the boy, who was concentrating very hard. He picked up the ball and threw it far, which is not the best way to tell a dog that the game is over.

Down below, Mino approached one of the henchmen guarding the treasure. He coughed slightly. "Excuse me for bothering you. Could you tell me the time, please? I can't see very well!"

The henchman had the face of a brute. It was a miracle that he had allowed the mole to finish his sentence. The guard leaned over and looked at the watch.

"I don't know how to tell time," he barked like an ogre.

A brute *and* a moron.

"Really? Oh, too bad. Well, it's not important," the little mole replied.

"Come on, Mino! Hurry up," Arthur prayed.

Alfred brought back the ball, wagging his tail. The dog definitely did not understand the tragedy that was unfolding before him. He only saw his ball and the game that went along with it.

Arthur, annoyed, grabbed the ball and threw it as hard as he could to the other end of the garden.

Well, that was the plan, anyway. Unfortunately, a tired arm and a light wind decided otherwise. The ball swerved off course and crashed through the living room window.

Inside, Davido jumped up, spilling coffee all over his beautiful cream-colored suit. He began yelling insults that pain transformed into gibberish.

Grandma hurried over, a towel in her hand, while Grandpa pretended to look bothered.

"Oh, I am so sorry! You know how it is! Children!" he said.

Davido grabbed the towel out of Grandma's hands and wiped himself off.

"No, thank goodness! I have not yet had the pleasure," he sputtered through clenched teeth.

"Ah! Children!" marveled Archibald. "A child is like a lamb that fulfills your life and, in my case, has saved it," he confessed.

"Can we leave the lambs alone and return to the business at hand?" suggested Davido. He pushed the papers that needed to be signed under Archibald's nose.

"Of course," Grandpa replied, looking at the papers. He needed to find another way to buy more time. "First let me make you another cup of coffee," he said, standing.

"Don't bother," Davido replied, but Grandpa pretended to be deaf and headed for the kitchen.

"The coffee comes from central Africa. You are really going to like it!"

Maltazard still had his arms outstretched, facing the jubilant crowd.

"My faithful soldiers!"

The crowd fell silent.

"The hour of glory has arrived," cried their sovereign in a voice that would freeze your blood.

The henchmen screamed with joy. You had to wonder whether they understood what was being said or were blindly obeying the sign that Darkos held up on which was written the word "Applause." But since most of them couldn't read, they were happy just to cheer.

Maltazard waited for silence and continued his speech. "I

promise you wealth and power, grandeur and eternity!"

The henchmen cheered again, not really understanding what their king was promising and what they would never be receiving. There was little chance that he would share any wealth and power, much less grandeur and eternity.

"We are now going to invade and conquer all the lands that were promised to us," he added, sending the crowd into a frenzy. This they understood, and mosquitoes and henchmen alike stamped their feet with excitement at the size of the mission being entrusted to them.

Mino's mission was much less ambitious. He simply had to read the time on the watch Arthur had given him. He plucked up his courage and tried again.

"Excuse me—it's me again," he said politely to the henchman. "I'd like to give this to you," he added, handing him the watch.

The henchman was so stupid, it was very unlikely that he would know what a gift was. Mino did not give him time to think—that could take hours. He quickly strapped the watch around the henchman's wrist.

"There! It looks very good on you," he said.

The henchman looked at the watch for a moment, like a pineapple would look at a television.

"What am I supposed to do with this? I don't know how to tell time."

"No problem! When you want to know what time it is, all you have to do is hold up your arm in the direction of someone who does know how. Me, for example. Lift your arm—you'll see, it's easy."

The henchman, dumber than a fish that has never seen a hook, listened to Mino and raised both his arms. The little mole could finally see the time on the watch from a distance that was comfortable for his eyes.

"My goodness! Five minutes past noon," he cried in a panic, and ran off toward his levers, leaving the henchman planted like a scarecrow.

On the surface of the earth, Arthur was still waiting for the little mole to work his magic. But nothing had happened yet, and Arthur began to despair.

Down below, Mino was trying his best. The animal made his calculations as fast as possible—and you have no idea how fast a mole can calculate. He pulled on several levers, which immediately adjusted the position of several rubies. As a result, the light, which had been illuminating the pyramid, slowly began to fade without anyone realizing it. Everyone in this world was absorbed by Maltazard's speech, which he ended with the following words: "Let the festivities begin!"

The army screamed with joy. They threw their weapons into the air in perfect unison and, for a few moments, as swords and knives spun and glittered above them, the show was impressive. Its end was less so, however. Weapons fell every which way, raining down on the soldiers. The wounded numbered in the dozens.

Maltazard rolled his eyes, appalled by the stupidity of his army.

Mino took advantage of the temporary chaos to pull one last lever. All of a sudden, the light came together and was transformed into a magnificent red beam. It burst out of the top of the pyramid and climbed directly toward the outside world.

The audience let out an admiring "Oooohhh!" They obviously thought this new play of light was part of the show. "What a beautiful red" was heard here and there.

Mino pulled a lever and the beam intensified. Like a bolt of lightning, it sliced through the sky of Necropolis.

"It's magnificent, O divine sovereign," rejoiced Darkos, applauding quietly in order not to drown out the clamoring crowd that idolized his father.

Maltazard had no idea what was happening, but he didn't want to admit it.

In the middle of the garden, a magnificent red ray shot out of the ground and climbed practically to the sky. Arthur screamed with joy and threw himself down so that he could look into the hole.

Alfred, who had succeeded in finding his ball, also came

over to investigate. Arthur thrust his hand into the hole, but his arm was not long enough to reach into the cavern.

Mino looked up and saw Arthur's shadow at the edge of the opening. Maltazard had also seen these shadows, and even if he did not really understand what was happening, he could still feel the impending danger.

"We must find the idiot responsible for this! Arrest him at once," he screamed at the guards who were positioned around the hall.

Arthur scratched his head. "I have to come up with an idea, Alfred! Right away!" the boy said as he looked at his dog.

Alfred pricked up his ears, as if he wanted the statement repeated.

Arthur sighed. There was nothing he could learn from this dumb dog. All he knew how to do was chase after the ball he was holding in his mouth.

Arthur paused. He had an idea.

"The ball! Of course!" he shouted. "You have saved my life, Alfred! Give me your ball!"

Alfred was thrilled. His master did want to play after all! He seized the ball and took off to the other end of the garden, his tail wagging happily as Arthur ran after him.

Arthur took off after his dog, but with only two legs against four, he could not catch him.

**   *   *

Meanwhile, the guards had regrouped and were marching toward Mino, spears at the ready. Mino trembled with fear, desperately searching for a way to defend himself.

"Alfred, STOP!" yelled Arthur, as he had never yelled before in his life, so loud that he hurt his throat. It was not exactly a shout that could kill, but it could certainly paralyze.

Alfred stopped cold in his tracks, transfixed by this awful cry that seemed to come from deep inside his master, as if a monster were living within him. He opened his jaws, the ball fell to the ground, and Arthur picked it up.

"Thanks," the boy said to him, once again calm, patting him on the head.

This was one game of catch that Alfred was not likely to forget.

CHAPTER
15

Mino was not likely to forget this day, either, since it was beginning to look like it would be his last.

The guards were massed in front of him, and Mino, as a last recourse, assumed a position of self-defense, Bruce Lee–style, mole version.

"Watch out," Mino warned, his hands in front of him. "I can be bad!"

Maltazard, fuming, pulled out the magic sword that he had stolen from Selenia. He swung the sword with a broad gesture and threw it, with all his might, in Mino's direction.

Although the mole had bad eyesight, his other senses were excellent, and he could tell there was a missile flying directly at him. Mino jumped slightly to the right. The blade planted itself noisily in the stone a few inches from Mino's contorted face.

Maltazard was furious at having missed his target, especially in front of his son.

"Seize him!" he shouted.

"I warned you! I am going to get angry," insisted Mino, stepping back carefully.

The henchmen laughed in disbelief. Too bad for them. A tennis ball, two hundred times bigger than they were, had just appeared in the tunnel above them. The object, as big as a meteorite to them, blocked the light from the surface, and the henchmen looked up to see this shadow rolling down on them. They didn't have long to wonder.

Barely a second later, the ball landed with a crash in the middle of the henchmen.

Maltazard bent over his balcony in a speechless fury.

"Arrest that ball," he cried.

The henchmen couldn't hear him. They were being swept away like dead leaves. With each bounce, the giant ball crushed, destroyed, and mowed down everything in its path.

Straws and pipes flew in all directions, like bowling pins. Released from the elaborate system of pipes, water now flowed from dozens of holes in the cistern. The square was full of sudden geysers that spit water released from the two enormous tanks. The torrent, which before had been pouring only into the tunnel to the Minimoy village, now was released to flow through the entire underground.

The ball rolled and bobbed on the water as far as the entrance to the tunnel, where it got stuck in the hole and began to block it, like a bathtub stopper. Very quickly, water filled the whole square, causing panic in the army of henchmen.

"Do something," Maltazard ordered his son. Darkos was at a loss.

Mino didn't have any idea what to do, either. He had climbed into the saucer holding the treasure and hid himself between two rubies. Now the water lifted the saucer and its treasure, and the little plate climbed gently inside the pipe that led to the surface.

Mino was completely terrified. Drifting on the surface of the water is not really a mole specialty, and our little friend quickly felt sick to his stomach.

The spectacle he saw before him was disastrous. Water had conquered the great square of Necropolis, carrying off the small merchants' stalls in all directions.

Some mosquitoes had remained on the ground and were already in water up to their saddles. Others flew around the royal hall, which now had no exits that were not completely underwater.

The henchmen who fell into the water sank very quickly, thanks to their heavy armor.

Entire sections of wall, eaten away by the water, collapsed into the square, causing monstrous waves. The same waves carried off the little groups of huts that came crashing into the palace walls, under Maltazard's balcony.

The sovereign saw this catastrophe climbing quickly toward him. Soon it would engulf his balcony. He couldn't believe it.

How could that little nothing of a mole cause such a cataclysm? How could an empire as powerful as his own fall so easily?

Sometimes all it takes is one grain of sand to stop a huge machine, a small stone to fell a giant, and a few courageous men to start a revolution. He would have known that if he had read *The Great Book of Ideas*, as Mino had advised him to do a hundred times. Commandment two-hundred and thirty would have reminded him that "the smaller the nail, the more it hurts when it is in your foot."

Maltazard understood the lesson now, but it was too late. He was lost, destroyed, just like his kingdom.

The water had now reached the balcony, and there were no longer many options for him. He chose the first one that came to mind: he jumped onto a mosquito.

The henchman who was piloting it was obviously very proud to have his master aboard but, as he soon discovered, there can only be one captain on any ship.

Maltazard grabbed the henchman and carelessly threw him overboard. The poor pilot didn't even have time to cry out before tumbling straight down into the tumultuous water.

Maltazard took the mosquito's reins, which were a little small for him, and prepared to leave.

"Father?" cried Darkos.

Maltazard pulled on the reins and stopped his mosquito.

His son was on the balcony, looking lost, up to his knees in water. "Don't abandon me, Father," he said in a voice that was almost childlike.

Maltazard moved in front of him, hovering.

"Darkos! I appoint you commander of all my armies and all these lands," his father said in a solemn voice.

Darkos was only vaguely flattered by this, for in order to take advantage of his new appointment, it would have been better to be dry. He extended his hand toward his father, hoping for a small spot on the back of the mosquito.

"And a captain never leaves his ship," his father added, annoyed at having to remind him of the most basic military rule.

Maltazard pulled on the reins, did an about-face, and disappeared into the vaulted sky of Necropolis.

Darkos, disappointed, bruised, and abandoned, lowered his head. He noticed that the water had already reached his waist and that his face was reflected in the water. He looked at the tired face rapidly rising toward him, like a brother looking to find him. This thought made him smile. Immediately, his reflection put on the same smile. Darkos was very moved by this. It was the first time that anyone had ever approached him with a smile.

It would also be the last. His reflection came closer and gave him a kiss good-bye.

Arthur was still stretched out on the grass, his ear planted to the ground so he could hear the gurgling sound rushing through the belly of the earth. The little hole into which he had tossed the ball still remained desperately empty, and Arthur began to wonder whether he had failed in the last part of his mission.

After having crossed the Seven Lands at a height of half an inch, fought henchmen, married a princess, found his grandfather and a treasure, he felt that to fail so close to the end would be too terrible. There was a kind of injustice here that Arthur could not allow. Why would his good fortune, which up to now had accompanied him, fail so suddenly? The thought gave him new courage, and once again he bent over the little hole. He clearly heard the water gurgling. The fact that it was getting louder meant only one thing: the level of the water was rising!

Arthur peered into the hole once more.

Suddenly, an object glistened. The first ruby at the top of the pyramid had just found the light. Little by little, the saucer rose, carried by the water, and the pyramid became increasingly illuminated.

Arthur was amazed and astounded. He had tears in his eyes.

His mission had been a success. A perilous mission, during which he had risked his life a hundred times, braving all kinds of dangers. An adventure that had forced him to go beyond anything he knew about himself. A path that he had begun as a small boy and that he had finished as a young man.

Arthur reached out his hands and caught the saucer full of rubies. He gazed at the treasure for a moment, the way a student looks at his diploma at the end of the school year.

The audience congratulated him by wagging its tail and barking its compliments.

Arthur hurried into the garage and turned on the bright fluorescent light, which hesitated a moment, as always, before working. The boy gently placed the saucer on the table and rummaged through the drawers of the workbench. Finally he found what he was looking for: a magnifying glass.

Arthur carefully examined the pyramid of rubies, in search of a little mole.

"Mino?" whispered Arthur. He knew his normal voice would sound monstrous to a Minimoy.

Mino had heard, but this strange noise worried him. How would he be able to recognize his friend Arthur, now that the tone of his voice had become so low? The little mole plucked up his courage and decided to show himself. As he scrambled free of the rubies, he slipped on a wall of glass and realized that the lens reflected a giant eye, bigger than a planet.

Mino let out a shriek and fell into the rubies, which is much better than fainting into oranges.

Half the Minimoy people had their hands and backs pressed against the door when they realized that the water pressure wasn't getting stronger anymore. In fact, it had started to weaken. Miro announced the good news, putting his ear to the door to listen.

The king stopped pushing but still did not dare to remove his hands.

Palmito asked fewer questions. He stepped back a few steps and stretched hugely, cracking his back. He had probably been responsible for two thirds of the work.

The king, alone with his hands on the door, began to feel a little ridiculous.

"You can let go, Father! I think it will hold," his daughter said, amused.

The sound of the water was receding, like a bad memory.

Miro opened the little window located at eye level and peeked outside. "The water is gone! Arthur and Archibald have succeeded," cried the mole.

The news was greeted with unparalleled joy, and hundreds of little hats were thrown into the air to the sound of screams, cries, songs, and various kinds of whistling. Everything that made it possible to express the joy of being alive was heard at that moment.

Selenia threw herself into her father's arms. Huge tears rolled down her cheeks and, at the same time, she burst into uncontrollable laughter.

Betameche was intoxicated by all the hands that wanted to shake his. He made sure to say thank you to everyone. The entire Minimoy people were jubilant and they spontaneously began to sing their national anthem.

Miro watched all of this wistfully, for his heart wasn't fully in it. The king approached and placed an arm on his shoulders.

He understood the unhappiness that was preventing Miro from celebrating.

"How I would have loved to have my little Mino here, to enjoy this spectacle!" Miro said sadly.

The king felt great sympathy for his friend. There was nothing to do, given the situation, and even less to say. But a new noise was beginning to disturb the celebration, stronger even than the noise of the water.

The ground began to tremble slightly and the ceremony immediately came to a halt. Worry could again be seen on everyone's faces.

The trembling of the ground grew more pronounced, and several chunks of earth fell from the ceiling, like bombs falling from the sky, that exploded, making huge craters.

Who other than a demon would attempt to destroy the vault over the city?

A jolt, much stronger than the others, detached an enormous stone from the ceiling.

"Watch out," cried Miro.

The Minimoys scattered, leaving the enormous stone to dig a hole in the ground in a cloud of dust. The shock was so violent that the king fell back.

At last the trembling stopped and a gigantic multicolored tube appeared from the ceiling, descending to the ground.

The king could not believe his eyes. *What diabolical thing has that demon Maltazard invented now?* he wondered.

The impressive tube steadied itself and, since it was transparent, it was now clearly possible to observe a ball sliding down the inside, toward them.

"A ball of death," cried Betameche.

That was all that was needed to cause total panic.

Selenia was the only one who stayed calm. The horrible tube reminded her of something . . . what was it? "It's a straw," she cried suddenly, smiling from ear to ear. "It's one of Arthur's straws!"

The ball finished its descent, hit the ground, and rolled to the side. It was Mino the mole! He stood up, aching all over, and spit the dust out of his mouth. He held Selenia's sword tightly in his arms, having rescued it from the wall before hiding in the pile of rubies.

"My son!" cried Miro, overcome with emotion.

"My sword!" rejoiced Selenia, crazy with happiness.

Miro ran to his son and hugged him tightly.

The Minimoy people, covered with dust, once again shouted for joy.

The king approached Miro and his son.

"All's well that ends well," he said happily, not at all sorry that the adventure was finally over.

"Not just yet," replied Selenia with authority.

She left the little group and walked to the center of the square, where the rock of the ancients stood. She brandished her sword and, in a single movement, planted it in the stone. The stone closed immediately, imprisoning the sword forever.

Selenia let out a sigh of relief. She glanced at her father who, with a nod of his head, indicated his approval. This adventure had taught her many things—especially one, which was essential for being a good queen and for succeeding in life in general. She had learned wisdom.

Very gently, the straw rose like a silent rocket, leaving the village square.

CHAPTER
16

Arthur pulled up the straw and checked to make sure that Mino was no longer inside. He placed a small stone over the hole he had made and recovered the saucer filled with rubies.

Archibald had run out of ways to stall for time. His hands were covered with ink and he was toying with his pen, which he had separated into three parts.

"It's incredible! This pen has never let me down before! And now, at the worst moment, when these important papers are to be signed, it falls apart!" Grandpa explained talkatively. "It was a Swiss friend who gave it to me and, as you probably know, the Swiss are not only specialists in clocks and in chocolate but they also make excellent pens!"

Davido, exhausted and suspicious, stuck his own fancy pen under Archibald's nose.

"Here! This one comes from Switzerland, too! Now, sign!

We've lost enough time as it is."

The landlord would not tolerate any more diversions. You could see it in his face.

"Ah? What? Yes, of course," mumbled Archibald, who had run out of ideas. He tried to gain a few more seconds by admiring the pen. "Magnificent! And . . . does it write well?"

"Try it yourself," Davido answered shrewdly.

Archibald had no other choice. He signed the last paper.

The landlord immediately grabbed it from his hands and put it in his file.

"There! Now you are the owner," said Davido, his expression somewhat strained.

"Wonderful!" answered Archibald, who knew that it wasn't so simple. He had filled out all the papers, but he had not paid the principal.

"So—the money!" Davido demanded, holding out his hand.

He knew that this was his last chance to steal the property. The deed would be invalid until Archibald had paid the sum due, and Davido was almost certain he did not have it. The old man looked at the two policemen on either side of Davido with a beseeching smile. Unfortunately, the two representatives of the law could not do much for him.

Davido felt the wind change direction in his favor. It was already a miracle that the old man had reappeared at the last moment. There could not be two miracles in the same day.

Davido opened the file, grabbed the deeds, and prepared to tear them up. "No money . . . no documents, no house," said the evil landlord.

The front door opened, and everyone turned toward it with the natural curiosity you have when you are waiting for a miracle.

On this occasion, the miracle was very polite. He entered by the door and wiped his feet before crossing the room.

Arthur came up to the table, where the audience was waiting for him with bated breath. He carefully placed the saucer full of rubies in front of Archibald.

Grandma held back her emotions, Grandpa his admiration. As for Davido, he held his breath. Was it possible?

Arthur was beaming with happiness.

Archibald rejoiced. He would finally be able to enjoy himself a little. "Well," he said, looking at the rubies, "good accounts make good friends. That is commandment number fifty-nine. . . ."

He chose a ruby, the smallest one. "That should cover it. Now you are paid!" he said, placing the tiny stone in front of Davido, who was mesmerized.

The two policemen breathed a sigh of relief. They were quite pleased by this happy ending.

Grandma placed a small jewelry box on the table. She picked up the saucer and emptied the rubies inside.

"They will be safer in here, and, besides, I have been look-ing for this saucer for four years," she said with humor, picking it up.

Archibald and Arthur laughed. Not Davido. Davido was not laughing at all.

"Sir, I bid you good-bye," said Archibald, standing up and indicating the exit.

Davido felt as though his legs had been cut out from under him. He could barely stand.

The two policemen saluted Arthur's grandparents by put-ting their hands to their caps and heading toward the door.

Davido, devastated, felt his nerves snap, one after the other. A nervous tic appeared at the corner of one eyelid and his eye began to wink, as if it were about to pass out. The road that leads from hatred to madness is not very long, and Davido now seemed ready to follow its path.

He opened his jacket and took out a pistol, a gesture that left no doubt as to its meaning.

"Nobody move," he cried.

The two policemen reached for their weapons, but Davido's madness had made him very sharp.

"Nobody, I said," he shouted again, even louder than before.

The others were speechless. No one had imagined that this villain would go so far.

Davido took advantage of the general astonishment to slip

the little box full of rubies under his arm.

"This is exactly what I was hoping for," he gloated.

"Is that why you absolutely had to have our property?" asked Archibald, who was beginning to understand.

"Of course! The desire for wealth! Ever and always." He laughed with a crazed look on his face.

"How did you know that our garden hid such a treasure?" Grandpa asked, mystified.

"It was you who told me, you stupid idiot," said Davido excitedly, his weapon still pointed at them. "One evening we were both in the Two Rivers bar. We were celebrating the end of the war, and you shared your stories of bridges and tunnels, of Africans, big and small, and of treasure! Rubies that you had brought back from Africa and carefully buried in the garden. They were so well hidden that you couldn't remember where. That made you laugh, but I have cried every night since then! I could not rest, knowing that you were sleeping peacefully on top of a treasure without even knowing where it was!"

"I am sorry to have disturbed your sleep so much," Archibald replied, as cold as ice.

"It's not important! Now that I have the treasure I can catch up on my sleep. You are the one who will never rest again," Davido assured him, beginning to step back toward the door.

"Davido, it was not the treasure that prevented you from

sleeping. It was your own greed."

"Well, today my greed is satisfied, and I promise you I will sleep well. I am thinking of the Caribbean. Africa is not really my style," replied the villain.

What he did not see was the five spears of the Bogo-Matassalai, now aimed at his back.

"Money doesn't buy happiness, Davido. That is one of the first commandments, and you will learn it soon enough," said Archibald. He was pained to see this poor madman fall into a trap that he himself had unwittingly set.

Davido took another step back and froze. He could feel the five lances pressing into his back, and he realized that his luck was changing again, like storm clouds rolling into a clear sky.

The two policemen jumped forward as he stood, paralyzed with fear, and disarmed him quickly.

The African chief recovered the jewelry box while the policemen handcuffed Davido and pushed him toward the door without time to say another word. Not even "farewell."

The Bogo-Matassalai chief gave Archibald the jewelry box.

"Next time, be more careful where you put the gifts you are given," said the chief with an enormous smile.

"It's a promise," replied Archibald. He was smiling, but he had learned his lesson.

Arthur ran into the arms of his grandma and took advantage

of some well-earned cuddling.

Meanwhile, out in the garden, Arthur's mother was slapping herself, not very hard, but still slapping. She knew it was the only thing that could wake her. Her husband came up and slipped his arm behind her back to help her sit up.

The first thing that she saw, upon opening her eyes, was Davido, handcuffs on his wrists, being thrown into the police car by the two officers.

Arthur's mother knit her brow, convinced that she was still in a dream.

"Are you feeling better, dear?" her husband asked gently.

She did not respond right away. She was waiting to see if the police car, with its sirens blaring, would fly up into the air.

The car raised a lot of dust, but it remained wisely on the road.

She was really in reality.

"Yes. Much better," she responded finally, as she stood and straightened her dress. She looked at all the holes her husband had made around her in the garden. "Everything is very good," she continued vaguely. She had obviously not completely come to, and her various falls must have rattled her brain.

"I'm going to straighten up a bit," she said, as if she were in the kitchen. She grabbed her shovel and began filling up the holes.

Her husband watched her, helpless. He sighed and sat down at the edge of one of the holes. There was nothing to do but wait and hope that his wife's condition was temporary.

CHAPTER
17

One week had passed since the amazing adventure. The garden was almost as good as new, the gravel in the driveway had been raked, the windows repaired, and the electricity and telephone turned on again.

The only difference was the delicious smell that was floating through the kitchen window.

Grandma lifted the cover of the pot. It had been simmering for hours and smelled absolutely wonderful. This probably explained why Alfred the dog was sitting quietly next to the stove.

Grandma dipped her wooden spoon into the pot, then took a tiny taste. Given the smile of satisfaction that appeared on her face, there could be no doubt: it was ready. She lifted the dish with the help of two towels and headed for the dining room.

"Ahh," everyone hummed with pleasure.

Archibald pushed the bottles aside to make room for the

beautiful new dish. "Oh! Giraffe neck! My favorite," he exclaimed.

Immediately, his daughter began to get up from the table, but her husband stopped her in mid-flight. She had recovered, but she was still somewhat fragile.

"I'm only joking," Grandpa guffawed.

Grandma served, and the delicious aroma of beef stew filled the room. Everyone was served—Arthur's mother, Arthur's father, the two policemen, the five Bogo-Matassalai—and they all waited politely until the mistress of the house finished going around the table.

The last plate was filled, but one chair was empty.

"Where is Arthur?" asked Grandma suddenly. She had been so busy with her stew that she hadn't noticed he was gone.

"He went to wash his hands. He'll be right back," Archibald replied.

Arthur had not really gone to wash his hands. He was upstairs. He came out of his grandma's room, the famous key in his hand, and tiptoed down the hall, making sure, this time, that Alfred wasn't following him.

There was no chance of that. On beef stew day, Alfred was never more than a few feet away from the kitchen.

Arthur arrived at the door to his grandfather's study and slipped the key into the lock.

The room was full again. The desk had been put back in its place. Each trinket, each mask, had found its nail and once again cluttered the room. The books also had the pleasure, once again, of piling on top of each other.

Arthur moved slowly, as if to prolong his pleasure. He touched the cherrywood desk, the large buffalo-hide trunk, and all the masks he had loved to play with before this story began. He glanced up at the banner that read WORDS OFTEN HIDE OTHER WORDS, which had started him on his adventure. He felt happy and sad all at the same time.

He opened the window and let summer fill the room. He put his elbows on the windowsill and sighed as he looked at the big oak tree and the garden gnome under it. Above, in the azure sky, a pale crescent moon offered itself timidly to the sun.

"Only eleven more moons, Selenia . . . eleven more moons," he said.

Arthur remained in the silence for a moment, hoping that an echo might send him a response. But none came. All he could hear was the whisper of a breeze in the leaves of the big oak.

Arthur kissed the palm of his hand, then blew on it to show it the path to take.

The kiss danced in the direction of the oak tree, passing nimbly through its branches and landing on Selenia's cheek.

The little princess was sitting on a leaf, looking up at Arthur in the window. A tear slid down her cheek.

"I'll be with you soon," whispered Arthur, with an air of melancholy.

Selenia knew he could not hear her, but she answered anyway.

"I'll be waiting."

WHERE ARTHUR'S SPELLBINDING FANTASY ADVENTURE BEGINS!

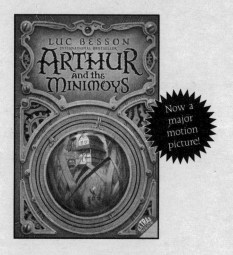

ARTHUR AND THE MINIMOYS
Hc 0-06-059623-6 · Pb 0-06-059625-2

In the first book of Arthur's incredible tale, his backyard seems perfectly ordinary—that is, until he discovers a whole world hiding in the grass: the world of the Minimoys. This tribe of tiny people is Arthur's only hope to save his home and his grandfather— and he might be *their* only hope as well.

Don't miss the 3-D animated movie based on both of Luc Besson's books!

 HarperTrophy®

An Imprint of HarperCollins*Publishers*

www.harpercollinschildrens.com